TRANSITION

TRANSITION

Book Three of the Narrator Cycle

Ian Patterson

Book Cover & Illustration by Barış Şehri: https://www.sehribookdesign.com/

Editing by Emil Ottoman: https://emilottoman.substack.com/

Proofreading by Colleen Reimer

Paperback ISBN: 979-8-9909170-4-0

eBook ISBN: 979-8-9909170-5-7

— First published edition, 2026 —

For anyone who ever wanted to stop.
This book is for you.
Keep going.

"Once upon a time, I dreamt I was a butterfly, fluttering hither and thither, to all intents and purposes a butterfly. I was conscious only of my happiness as a butterfly, unaware that I was myself. Soon I awaked, and there I was, veritably myself again. Now I do not know whether I was then a man dreaming I was a butterfly, or whether I am now a butterfly, dreaming I am a man."

Zhuangzi

One

Micah

"I tried to kill myself last year."

Micah says this while rolling a lit cigarette between his fingers, a smile on his lips, a flippant statement made with the reckless abandon of someone certain to be misunderstood. That the meaning will be lost on the beautiful face he's speaking to. *What was his name again? Michael? Vincent?* The dark eyes of the other man squint, and his mouth quirks upward at one corner.

Alpha station—where people come together. Micah hears the advertisement again and grimaces. There is a particular loneliness in communicating with mostly non-native speakers. Then again, there's a different loneliness in communicating with native speakers too.

"Are you... hunter, then?" His English is thick and slow, the corners rounded by a heavy foreign accent.

"Yes, of experiences and meaningless life lessons, mostly."

Oh Micah, how true these words are. I see your inner self on display. I see you running across the sand, striving to learn. What are you? Why are you? I want to know.

The brows of his companion crinkle together. *Was it Liu? Was that his surname? He just said it, why do I never listen? Was it Hsieh?* Micah takes a swig from his warming bottle of beer and crowns it with a long drag from his bummed cigarette. *Fuck it, I wouldn't have remembered tomorrow anyways.*

"You cannot hunt here," his companion responds after some time, clearly confused.

Fuck, this is dismal. We're in the middle of space on a mechanical bubble of artificial gravity and reprocessed air, flying around in the orbit of a home world all of us want to forget. The beer we're drinking is probably, somehow, made from our own recycled piss. No, of course there isn't hunting here.

"Look, did you want to come back to my place tonight?" Micah crushes the butt of his cigarette into a tray overflowing with them. *It's cramped, poorly lit, and mostly covered by a bed too small for two, just like yours is, I'm sure.*

The other man cocks his head. Idioms never translate well.

"Do you. Want to. Fuck me? I am ready to leave." Micah speaks each word forcefully, but stops short of making any obscene gestures to make sure his meaning is understood. Nearby heads turn in the cramped bar. A few people even eagerly raise their hands.

Anonymous Liu, or Hsieh, or whatever it is grins and nods. Micah leads him from the crowd.

Curious, I follow him closer. I want to see things through his eyes.

We walk the corridor back to my room, abandoned now but for the chittering of rats in the darkness. They'd infested the station, riding the coattails of human civilization, eating our detritus. In time, they warped like us to become something different, something new. The size of cats, skin strained from cancerous mutations, they're best left alone.

Shafts of artificial light from circles set in the ceiling punctuate the hallway, bastions of clarity that make our drug-strained pupils scream. Under their gaze, we squint and smile at each other. In the inky black between, we giggle, stumble, and fly. Our balance lost to booze, a few lines of Luna, and the fucking reduced grav they switch to every evening. With the ground holding us less firm, our steps become bounding leaps. We are unmoored in the darkness, and found again in the light.

He's pretty, or the cocktail in my gut is doing its job. Fresh-faced, shaved smooth, dark eyes and skin, he smells like a bloom of honeysuckle—an intoxication in itself. When you're inebriated, your brain blurs edges to find symmetry and lessen the mental load, so everyone looks prettier. The drunken pillow talk from an old lover traces its groove in my memory.

We enter another pillar of light. I turn to find his face different than I remembered in the darkness. Lighter skin, a close-cut beard, twinkling blue eyes squint against the sudden illumination.

My smile falters.

Fuck, was I remembering a different night?

A different person?

The darkness consumes us again. In it, I try to count the people I've slept with, to place their faces in a timeline, but I keep getting it wrong and revising it. Is it still called loneliness if you fill the void every night? No, it's only loneliness if it comes from the lonely region of France. Otherwise it's just called a sparkling coping mechanism.

When the light breaks in again, he's changed.

Pale and skinny, with lanky hair.

This isn't right. Something is wrong.

I drop his hand and back away as adrenaline soars through me. My heart is a deer chased in the wilderness, thundering hooves in my chest. Fear chasing clarity into my brain like a sudden punch to the face.

His smile widens, impossibly huge.

I look down the hall. I need something real, something to anchor me.

I'm drifting.

I'm drunk.

This isn't real.

Under each lamp is a different reflection of me. They mirror my movements, backing away from a different person in each.

I whip my head around, and so do all of them.

In both directions.

What the fuck is happening here?

What the fuck is this?

"Is everything okay?" His voice is a pantheon. A cacophony of dialects, tones, and pitches. All of them familiar. It echoes—repeating, overlapping. Waves over waves.

I take a step backwards into the darkness, and he reaches for me. In my periphery, some other version reaches for some other me in every shaft of light. His hand draws near. So close. Almost touching mine.

I run.

I race into the void, hands outstretched to find the access hall I know is there. I sprint blindly into the pitch, bouncing high from the low gravity, guided by the squeals of rats as they scurry from me. I follow them, and when their noises echo off the walls, I know I've made it into the passageway.

Freedom. Escape.

Legs pumping, chest heaving.

And then, my ears are ringing and I'm lying on the ground.

I don't remember running into the low-hanging metal pipe. I won't see it until the next morning. Vertigo writhes inside me, and I vomit a torrent of sour-milk-smelling undigested booze and drugs and sadness. I taste the acid on my tongue before it splashes against the cold metal flooring, and then the true darkness takes me.

I stare out into the twinkling abyss of space through a full-height viewing window. In the thick, reinforced plastiglass,

I see a reflection of myself with softened edges. More a form than an image, my outline defined by the muted illumination of distant stars. When I move forward to touch it, the whole window pulls away like a curtain in my hand. Behind it is the gray static of background electromagnetic waves. Humming white noise fills my head. It builds and builds and builds.

I wake to fluorescent lights punching my eyeballs and the noise of small, scampering feet. My head pounds. I wince and push myself off the ground to a sitting position. It breaks the crust of dried puke and unleashes fresh waves of stomach acid, old beer, and rotting soy sauce. I rub the heels of my hands against my blurred eyes, and stare at a rat lapping up the pile of spew. Its tail is half-missing. Gray hair spills haphazardly from its too-large body. Swollen tumors stand out on its shoulder and belly.

"Fuck. What the hell happened last night?"

As if I was asking it, the rat looks up.

"Well, you ran into a pipe and knocked yourself out. I'd advise against it in the future."

The voice yanks me back into some semblance of sobriety, and I spin around to look down the hall. Electric pain ricochets through my brain and lances the backs of my eyeballs. There's no one there. What the fuck?

I see shafts of light.

I see the multiples of me.

I see a hand reaching.

I clamp my eyes shut as nausea fills my mouth with saliva.

"Hey, down here."

I look back and lock eyes with the rat. It's sitting on its haunches now, waving at me. A speck of vomit clings to its lower jaw.

"Yeah, that's right, I know, talking rat. Very surprising."

I stare at the thing dumbfounded. Was something laced in those lines of Luna? Did I actually break my brain? Am I dead? Is that what this is? I look around again at the same shitty, bright hall of the orbital station. The metal is as stained as I remember it, covered in half-removed graffiti and what might be blood. Dirty and dingy is a way of life up here.

"Can you talk? It's a lot more interesting if you respond, you know?"

I open my mouth, and close it again like a fish out of water. "Are you God?"

The rat laughs at me, a deep, knee-slapping, crying kind of laugh.

"God? I just ate your vomit, and you think I'm some magical deity come to visit you? That's rich."

"But you're...talking. Wait, are you like, an experiment or something?"

"Are you struggling to not call me a lab rat right now?"

"I mean, I know the science deck is working on something important, so it seems fairly reasonable to assume—"

"That I'm a science experiment?"

"I mean, it seems reasonable to assume, right?"

"Do you have a depth of experience with talking rats to draw on here?"

Have I offended it? What does it say about my flagging sanity that I'd feel bad if I offended it? Flagging? Not so sure, it might be fully gone by now. I did just ask the rat if it was God.

The rat sighs. "Maybe it's best if we don't talk about what I am."

"Oh, then what should we talk about? Have a little chat about the weather? It's really nice today, they must have turned up the heat a fraction of a degree because I'm only partially reminded that we're surrounded by an unlivable vacuum. I heard we're expecting solar flares by midday though, which will almost certainly affect my doom scrolling when it blacks out our communications network."

"You just woke up in a pile of your own vomit, and a rat is talking to you. Shouldn't you like, go back to your room or something? I don't know, take a shower? Maybe you haven't noticed, but you smell."

I open my mouth to make another witty response. The talking rat, or whatever is creating this sign of my own crumbling grasp on reality, is right. I need a shower, not more banter. Moving inch by inch, my hand on a nearby wall for support, I make my way to standing. My stomach does acrobatics, and I close my eyes and breathe. One foot in front of the other, I start the journey back to my room. The scratching of tiny rat feet follows me.

I'm too hungover for this shit.

The station is a continuous stream of people flowing in both directions. As I move down the halls, half blinded, shaky legged, and with a piercing headache, they rush around me, avoiding all contact. I must look pretty terrible. Some are uniformed officers dressed in their sharp military blues, always hurrying, and as I get closer to my room I see more white uniforms of the science crew. There are a few other civvies like me wandering the halls, obvious by their plain, brown jumpsuit, maybe making their way to a shift in the mess hall or janitorial.

None of them seem to notice there's a cat-sized rat following in my footsteps. Potentially, this is because it's Monday and most of them are at least slightly hungover, as evidenced by their bleary eyes and ruddy faces.

Everyone up here is required to work, it's part of the housing contract. Which doesn't mean the civilians aren't paying through their nose for a placement, we all are. It's hard to argue against when the only other option is to be part of the dockyards on Earth. At least up here, you don't have to build the seed ships that will eventually leave us all behind. I'd done my time down there, and thankfully escaped to this lap of *luxury*. And conveniently, being required to work also means it's damn hard to be out of a job. They just give you a different employment contract.

Allegedly, I should be working my shift in janitorial right about now. Which almost certainly means I will be receiving another angry voice memo from my supervisor. It was a new position after my boss at the bakery got me reassigned, where I'd only landed after my dream job as a bartender saw me drinking more than serving, and was equally as awful as my brief tenure in shipping and receiving. I'd already blown off half my shifts with claims of migraines. I'm not sure where I'll get reassigned after janitorial, but at this moment signs are certainly pointing to me finding out in the near future.

Do they just throw you out an airlock when you flunk out of shit-cleaning duty?

I look behind me, and hot on my heels is the same lumpy, partially haired creature from earlier. Shit. Maybe I could just claim I missed my shift because I was so concussed I thought a rat was talking to me? It would add a bit of flair to the usual, anyways.

"Stop following me, you lumpy, vomit-eating cretin."

"You're the one covered in the stuff. Also, you're making other people think you're crazy."

I look up in time to catch eyes with my elderly neighbor as she peers through a crack in the door. She closes it hurriedly. Great, now she knows I can talk to rats.

I turn the final corner to my room, and find a small crowd gathered in white uniforms outside the door. I furrow my brows, hoping it will unlock access to a deeper level of understanding, or at least make me look thoughtful, but the pinching movement sends pain stabbing through my temples. I close my eyes to shut it out, my hand coming up to ease the pain, and lose my balance. I fall sideways into the corridor wall.

What an entrance.

The medical professionals stare at me, collapsed against a wall and covered in dried vomit. I push myself back upright and smile at them. In my mind, it's a dashing smile which simultaneously transfers the knowledge that I am fully in control, not at all still drunk, did not suffer a concussion after a potential drug-fueled mental break, and am not now currently, nor have I ever been, associated with a talking rat. Unfortunately, it sends shooting pain through my temples again and a repeat of the previous falling episode.

"Christ, he's still hammered." I hear one of them say.

"We have got to get the bars to stop over-serving."

"Yeah, they should be the ones doing this."

"I mean, what, fifth one this morning already?"

"You should have seen the mess he woke up in," the talking rat says at my side, and I kick at it.

"Is he having a stroke? Just our luck."

"Why do we always get the fucked-up ones? Why can't they just be accidentally sleeping in or something?"

"Citizen, we came here for a health check as requested by your employer. Are you currently experiencing mental and/or physical duress which would require assistance? Please keep in mind, a full report will be made of this situation, including *bloodwork*, if so." One of the whites says, her eyes boring into mine.

"I'm fine. Just hit my head last night and need to lay down. Should be dancing by midday I'd bet," I say, meeting her unflinching gaze. When I blink, all of the white uniformed faces become hers. A copy of a copy of a copy.

Like a repeated image down a hallway.

Like a multitude of past lovers reaching for me at the same time.

Mouths impossibly wide.

Fear hits first, then overwhelming nausea.

I empty the contents of my stomach, which at this point just contains a large quantity of frothy yellow bile, onto the hallway between us. When I look back up, their faces have returned to distinct people again, each of them disgusted in their own uniquely personal way.

"Dammit, Frank, order a cleanup crew. God it smells awful. Look Mr.—" She looks at the datapad in her hands. "Mr. Angelos, with your permission I'm going to help you into your apartment and let your employer know you're sick today, but will contact them tomorrow. Do you consent?"

I almost had them believing I was alright, too. I grunt and make an affirmative hand gesture as another wave of nausea rolls over me. A firm hand grabs my right arm, and guides me into the room. The woman, whose eyes are ringed with something resembling compassion, which I then realize is pity, sits me down on my bed. She wipes my face down with a warm washcloth, and helps me remove my puke-stained clothing. I want to lean into her soft hands. I want her to tell me everything is going to be okay, I just made a mistake but so does everyone.

Only then do I remember my studio apartment is a wasteland littered with piles of crumpled clothing and teetering mountains of dirty dishes filled with decomposing scraps of food. Nothing quite like the welcoming, earthy smell of trash. I look around at the mess, and meet her eyes. "Sorry, I would have cleaned if I knew I was having company."

She rolls her eyes. "Please lay down, Mr. Angelos." With a soft pressure, she guides my shoulders down onto the mattress. I sink into it. When she turns off the lights in the room, I start to drift. The sound of scurrying, clawed feet picking up momentum across metal flooring echoes in the small space, and then with what I can only picture is an impossibly high jump on those tiny legs, the lumpen form of the rat lands at my feet. I kick out at him, I thrash, but it seems to lack physical form.

"UGH. Get out of here!"

"Trust me, that'd be harder to do than you realize."

I consider getting up and throwing it out, but at the thought of movement my stomach flips again, and I resign myself to staying immobile.

Why didn't any of the med staff see it? Did it slink in behind them? Before I can pursue this thought with some reasonable, probing questions —like, why is a rat talking to me, what the fuck happened last night, was that Luna laced, am I going insane—I pass out.

I dream of the docks. Of those hot, tiring days underneath the oppressive sun. Covered in that inescapable mixture of sweat and oil. It clogged my pores and ruined my complexion. No matter how much I tried to stay clean, to not let the docks get under my skin, to not let it infect me, it was an impossible task. That place gave everyone who worked there two things: acne, and the inescapable loneliness that comes from knowing you're at the end of the line.

We built ships, but none of us ever saw them. We saw the minutiae. The bolts that held it together. I wasn't skilled labor, I was a warm body who could swing a hammer, and understood things generally tightened when rotated to the right. And so, every day I did meaningless jobs with a shifting crew of other meaningless people.

My body became ugly with the work. My slender frame I had cultivated, mostly from an extreme avoidance of physical labor of any sort, disappeared. Muscles strained and bulged from tired shoulders, their deep lines carving down onto my chest and back. Abs rippled in tight, countable rows. In the mirror, I was an alien to myself.

I dreamed of the day the reporters came. All excited bustle, cameras angled to the skyline of the structure, framed heroically against the sky, and away from those of us working below. Except for one of them. He wandered down into our midst, a press badge hanging near the chasm of his low buttoned shirt.

Most of all, I remember his smell. A clean scent, tinged with vanilla. It cut through the machine grease of our world. It cleared my sinuses, and made me look up. He was pretty, but not overly so. There was a sadness in his eyes, a common understanding, that made him beautiful. When he approached, one hand holding his camera, I stood up instinctively.

None of us said anything. There was a gravity to the situation that defied speech. The old cook stopped stirring his wok. The men set down their tools and stared. We were silent, all of us.

When he photographed me, I didn't smile. We were all dead men on a dying planet, building ships for those who would live. The man's camera sought truth, and so I let him see truth written in the twin tear tracks cutting through grease smudges that I did not wipe away. And he pulled the trigger.

Two

Not Micah

While the man sleeps, I observe the rest of the station. It hums with the day's activities, a series of inconsequential tasks repeated mindlessly. One person cleans a thing, so another can dirty it. One person cooks, so another can eat. Order, disorder. The same bustle in all of the worlds. From far enough away, humans resemble ants.

It was down close, granular, where it was all more interesting. Close-up, you could see their fullness, their motivations, their complexities and uniqueness. You could see their stories, the ones they told themselves, and the ones they tried not to. Or at least, it was that way for some of them. Others were just so many copies.

Rarely, something interesting would happen in the science hall, something new and novel I hadn't seen before. But then the scientists would ruin the excitement by studying the thing, debating its mechanisms, performing the same experiments to double check the results. Coming up with counter-hypotheses and debating statistical data from three different sides. I understand the method, but the tedium bored me. I wanted the eureka moments, the flash of non-normalcy and excitement. This is a crucible for survival. They should act accordingly.

There is a spark of brilliance here, on this station. The scientists study a strange DNA modification method. It allows them to drastically alter one body, using another body's DNA as guidance. To take one rat, and make it into another rat. But one of them dreams wider, in a way the mad always do, and runs simulations studying the use on humans. His colleagues would usually never agree to a study, a clear boundary the safe would never cross, but they're all driven by the need for it. Success means a chance at life, they think. The safe won't live long.

Passion is a lever I can use.

Three

Micah

Some great beast breathes out, its mechanical chest rattles all around me. I'm trapped inside it, swallowed whole. I can feel its hot breath tickle my face. It pings, pops, creaks. It builds to a roar quickly, and then settles. How has humanity settled in geosynchronous orbit but still hasn't made this god-awful electric heating any quieter?

The pressure on my body increases slowly as the station comes back to full gravity, pushing me deeper into the mattress with its invisible hands. Somehow, I've slept until the following morning. Light fades into existence, softening the darkness and giving shape to my room. My cell. The piercing pain in my head has settled to a dull throb I feel whenever I move my eyes. My hangover's half-resolved, but my mouth tastes like I was chewing on insulation foam dipped in sewage all night. I push myself up to sitting slowly, and hear the soft snoring of the black, lumpy thing near my feet pause briefly, and then resume.

Great, so that thing still exists.

I extract myself from the bed, careful not to wake the rat, and find my way over to the faucet, navigating the landmines of trash and discarded clothes along the way. As carefully as I can with shaking hands, I pull a cup from a haphazardly assembled art installation of dirty dishes. Through some miracle it doesn't all come tumbling down. I fill the cup, take a long, slow drink of water. The light in the room increases fractionally again, and I hear the sounds of waking in the rooms around me.

Yesterday was fucked. Grade A, brain-melting, reality-questioning bullshit. The kind of thing that will make a man stop and wonder: have I done too many drugs and am I now suffering a mental collapse? Are these just the worst fucking withdrawals of my life? There's a talking rat asleep on my bed, a string of words I never thought I'd put together, and I've seen things which make me fairly certain the real world and I are at odds with each other, if not teetering on all-out war. And yet, I'm also fairly likely to get sent to reassignment again today, and will somehow be required to function like a well-rounded member of society.

I turn to fill up the cup again, but semidistractedsemiconcussed, I move too fast and slam my hand into the teetering pile of dishes. Metal plates, bowls, cups, knives, forks, spoons of various sizes, and a pair of earrings I've been missing for a week fly across the room. They all clang like a child using pots and pans as their first drum set. I wince as electric pain stabs at my hungover brain.

My neighbor, a grumpy, stooped woman with more mass in her white hair than her bones, pounds her fist on the wall in irritation. I vaguely consider letting loose a symphony of thumps back, letting her know I don't give a good goddamn if she's experienced some discomfort, or that she saw me stumbling home yesterday, and she should probably just go ahead and die instead of using station resources, but I'm distracted by an elongated sigh from the foot of my bed.

The rat, who I'm starting to think needs a name at this point because I'm tired of referring to it that way, although it certainly wouldn't be the first to sleep over without one, is stretching. It strains its legs and arms outwards from its lumpy body, pushing them as far as it can, and then relaxes completely with a great sigh. It's such a human movement I feel a visceral urge to do the same thing. I quash it. I will not be taking my cues for relaxation from a rat which may or may not really exist.

"Alright, since you obviously didn't dissolve into thin air while I slept, what do I call you?" I say, walking back across the room and sitting on the bed again.

The rat yawns, and I force my mouth closed so I don't mimic him. "Always with the names, can't I just exist? Isn't that enough? Also, do you have any food in here?"

I look over at the scattered dishes on the floor, remnants of decomposing food still clinging to them. "A veritable feast." I say, motioning to them. "Now, as to the name. If you fail to provide one, I shall be forced to make one up for you. As much as I'd like to believe that you'll fade from existence, I'm starting to think you're part of a bigger, more fundamental break I'm having with reality fueled by copious drugs, withdrawals from copious drugs, or some mental wiring I've finally fried."

The rat plops off the bed and scurries over to lick the food greedily. The idea of his tiny tongue sliding over moldy food remnants ratchets up my latent nausea. I close my eyes and swallow it down.

"But, why?"

"Listen, this is an important step in the anthropomorphization of a sidekick, I've seen it enough times to know. Without a name, people can't properly place themselves in your ugly, scraggly, clawed feet."

The rat snorts. "Okay then, have at it I'd say. What's my name?"

"Bambi."

He pauses and turns around to stare at me. "Like the cartoon deer? I think you have the roles reversed. Thumper was the sidekick. Bambi was the one that got shot and survived. I see myself more as the Man, anyways."

"Sorry, you've given up the right to choose your own name now, and 'the Man' would be infinitely confusing given you're a rat. I will infer from this that you prefer male pronouns though."

"Another silly creation."

"Look, Bambi. I am not about to debate gender theory with you. It is entirely too early, I am still hungover, and I am largely convinced that you're an extension of myself—"

Another pounding on the wall from my elderly neighbor interrupts our conversation. Likely, she's upset that others do in fact exist and prefer talking instead of just staring judgmentally past doorframes.

"I hate that woman with my whole being. Anyways, you're reading too far into the name. It fits because you're as far removed from a beautiful, innocent fawn as I can imagine. Also, I won't get it confused in conversation with other people when I'm discussing the potentially invisible rat following me around. Which is truly a topic I can't wait to broach, first with a therapist, and then probably with anyone else who will listen."

"I'm not invisible, not really. I'm just good at distracting people so they think I'm not there."

"Oh, I didn't realize you were a ventriloquist. We'll add that to your resume, right there next to not a science experiment and not actually God. But can we come back to this fundamental understanding of your being *seen*. Which is an important thing to know so that people don't think I'm crazy."

"Well, that's easy—they will absolutely think you're crazy if you tell them about me."

"Let me remind you those are my decaying food remnants you're eating and I can just as easily take them away."

"Fine. Assume that I cannot be seen."

Next to my door, a small square screen the size of my hand chimes. A red light blinks in one corner. I roll my eyes and walk over to it, and press my thumb over the red light.

Automated message for MICAH ANGELOS. Your current employment contract has been terminated. Please proceed to the workforce center at your earliest convenience for reassignment.

The voice is shrill and metallic, knives dragged through circuitry. It's obviously trying to approach human, a designer somewhere worked hard at it, but it falls far short in the pacing, syncopation, tone, and you know, everything that might make it sound human. I navigate through menus and turn it back to *text-only*. A process I do every single time, but the damn thing hates me and just reverts. This is my Sisyphean boulder, and I will not stop carrying it to the top of the hill.

I sigh for the six hundredth time already this morning, and with irritation fueled procrastination, start to clean my room.

Casimir Petrov's sheer presence would make you believe Thracians did at one point walk the planet, and they were some bad motherfuckers. Muscles strain his too-tight, pressed maroon uniform. The color of administration. And who the hell presses their uniforms? Psychopaths. Even sitting down, his red-blonde ponytailed head towers over mine. He wears a small pair of wire frame glasses to read the computer screen in front of him, items which both look like they're in the immediate danger of being crushed by his massive, meaty palms.

"Civilian, you are presenting at reassignment. Again." His thick European accent sounds like it was pulled directly from the villain in a bad action movie.

"Seems that way," I say with a shrug of my shoulders, hoping my noncommittal response would infuriate Casimir. From the sudden clench of his square jaw, I imagine I'm successful.

He sighs, types a query into his keypad and squints at the computer. "90 days assigned janitorial department, you missing 39 days, no notice."

That seems like a high number. I mentally do the math—there was the nearly week-long bender after I started, several mornings of sleeping in and then just deciding to stay in bed scrolling on my datapad...there was a distinct time when I did try to go to work, but then decided staring out a window into the vastness of space was a better use of my time. Sure, 39, I'll take his word for it.

"Seems that way."

"Civilian, you are required working to preserve your habitation at this station. You are understanding this?"

"What?! Casimir, are you playing a trick on me? This entire time, I had no idea." I add in my best surprised pose—hand splayed across chest and eyebrows raised.

He scowls and presses a few more keys. "Computer presently determine your reassignment. Take a minute to processing."

"Ohhh, I wonder where you'll wind up this time," Bambi adds in from the corner of the room, rubbing his paws together. I ignore him.

"Casimir, darling, let me ask you something while we wait. Is your entire job to just press a button on the computer and read out the results? Doesn't this seem, I don't know, unnecessary? Like maybe, your life would be so much more fulfilling if I just spoke to the computer directly?"

"I am people person. I speak to people so computer not have to." Casimir delivers this line through a jaw clenched so hard I wonder if his teeth are made of metal from surviving the force of it. Then I hear one crack, a big one from the sound of it. Casimir doesn't react.

"And that seems like a very challenging role which must use the full range of your diverse skills. Now what if, instead of trying to chew and swallow your own teeth, you used those powerful hands and keypad of yours to place me into a similar position. Then I'll be on my merry way and you'll never need to reassign me ever again. You see, I think I've missed my true calling as an Administration chair warmer, and I am fully prepared to prove my dedication to the assignment."

"Careful, this one looks liable to punch you in the face," Bambi says from under my chair, and I shuffle my feet to kick at him.

Purple rage spills out from Casimir's maroon collared shirt, and inks across his face. Déjà vu. Have I experienced this before? I am almost entirely certain he's about to reach across the sheet metal desk and throttle me when the computer chimes and distracts him. He reads the monitor and scowls deeper.

"You are reassigning to science team."

"That doesn't sound like a downgrade."

The great ball of muscle shrugs. "It is determined best use of your *skillset.*"

"Who's the lab rat now?"

"That's a good joke Bambi, really. Quite highbrow stuff."

"What you say?" Casimir stands up and menaces at me.

"Shit, I was—never mind. Does that thing say what my role will be?"

"I'm sure you're qualified to be experimented on," Bambi mutters.

"Science team will choose this." Casimir grips the edges of the desk and I wonder how long it will maintain structural integrity.

The machine dings again, and it brings Casimir some great pleasure. A smile even turns at the corners of his mouth. It looks unfamiliar and painful to him, like bad gas. Has he smiled before? Or maybe this is one of those cliché villain smiles that they get right before they drop you into the tank of sharks?

Casimir puts his hands on his hips and laughs throatily, completing his villain arc. "You are banned from use of alcohol, and even approaching bar alert station security."

I slam my fist into the table between us and don't let my face betray how painful it is. "Oh goddamnit, that can't be legal!"

Casimir has a wolf's grin as he leans toward me across the table. "Civilian, we set the rules here."

I stand to leave, knowing any more argument would only give him more satisfaction. Bambi, hiding under my chair, pokes his mutant head out.

"What a charming individual, have you considered asking him out?"

"As soon as I find an airlock, I'm throwing you out of it."

"Hah, would like to see you trying this. New assignment starting tomorrow morning civilian, don't be late." Casimir calls after me.

"I'm going to be so fucking late," I say right before the automated door closes.

Walking aimlessly away from the reassignment meeting, my palms start to itch. It's the start of withdrawals certainly, from Luna or booze I'm not sure, but my guess is on the former. More importantly, it's barely midday, or whatever you call the liminal time on an orbiting space station where you can't directly see the sun but are told the relative time by clocks. I don't have anything to do until tomorrow. My stomach growls, and I course correct for the mess hall.

Being on station must be a somewhat similar experience to being stuck on a naval ship. We're each given a ration of food daily, and an allotment of extra ration cards to use throughout each month as needed. A variety of options are available in the mess hall, but the most popular things quickly run out between deliveries. This usually means after a few days we're all eating the same gruel, a brown paste that contains everything essential and nothing enjoyable.

My feet know the route. It's a body awareness that comes from walking the same halls constantly, more physical than memory. A trance-like drifting type of movement. I walk a series of passages, indistinguishable from each other, each with a distinct arrow at the end pointing to my goal. A right, another right, and another right, and one more to get me... wait, what the fuck?

Four right turns.

Four hallways.

Four signs.

I made a fucking circle.

And yet, I'm here.

I shake my head to clear the absurdity of it. Another withdrawal symptom?

From the smell, I timed my trip perfectly near a food delivery. Frying garlic and onion waft down the hall, carried on the auditory frontal assault of too many voices echoing inside a metal room. I walk into the chaos of lunch.

I've seen the photographs, I know the design of this tin room was lifted straight from the shopping mall food courts of the distant past. Vendors line the outside walls, long tables the inside courtyard, and everything is metal and bolted down. I can't imagine a place more hostile to human empathy. The far wall is entirely taken up by the largest viewing window on the entire satellite. The blue pearl of Earth hangs in view, beautiful and calm from this distance. It's only when you get much, much closer that the rampant pollution, erratically shifting climate, and disappointment of the human condition becomes visible.

I navigate the outer perimeter to the shops where Mandarin dominates the conversations. When the food delivery comes, most English speakers jovially search out their favorite burger and fries, or steak and potatoes, or some other asinine combination of salted meat and starch, but I crave the richness of spices.

So does my hangover.

I see Shi Tsai, ladle in one handle and wok in the other, working both rhythmically, and make my way to his shop. He catches my eye and smiles widely across the crowded aisle. I shoulder through the throngs of people, and reaching up under my shirt to the hidden sash I wear there, pull out two plastic ration cards. He grins out at me through the curls of Szechuan steam surrounding his stall.

"Big spender! What's the occasion?" He holds my gaze while still swirling the ladle and pot in an unbroken cadence. The aroma of peppers, garlic, and spring onion fried in the wonderful umami of sesame oil and soy sauce make my eyes water and stomach bark.

"New job, moving up in the world. Also I probably won't be able to trade my extras this month for anything illicit, so I might as well enjoy something."

Shi chuckles. "New job? Again? If you stand too proud against the wind, it will break you. Better to bend with it. What will you get?"

I nod thoughtfully. Shi's basically a saint in my eyes, I'd never mock him for giving me a heavy dose of conventional wisdom. Shit, I probably need it. He cooks the best food anyways and I certainly wasn't going to lose that lifeline.

"Serving of everything, Mr. Tsai, if you please."

He cackles and builds a tray for me. A spoonful of perfectly white rice, then fragrant fried greens with big chunks of chili and ginger, and two scallion pancakes on top with a beautiful drizzle of something warm and dark. Then a large bowl of beef noodle soup, and with a wink, an extra scoop of chili oil. Seeing the tremor in my hand when I give him the ration cards, he tuts and meets my gaze.

"Take care, Micah. You're too young for this." Shi shakes his hands with the ration card back at me. "First man takes a drink, then drink takes a drink, then drinks takes man."

"Thanks Shi, I know." There are tears in my eyes quicker than I can stop them, and I wipe them away with the back of my hand. How long has it been since anyone showed any sort of real care for me? How fucking lonely am I for crying when a cook is kind to me?

"If I also recite traditional proverbs will it make you tear up?" Bambi says from somewhere under a crowd of legs. I ignore him and send a prayer to whatever god is listening that he gets stepped on.

Shi holds my gaze for a moment too long, concern etched on his brow, and then smiles again to greet the next customer.

I navigate the maze of people, and find a rare seat near the port window.

"You may have noticed I didn't respond to you back there. That's because one, fuck you for mocking Shi, and two, I appear absolutely insane talking to an *invisible* thing. Recent events have made me start to question my sanity already, and the last thing I need is societal agreement on it before I've reached my own conclusion."

"Would it help if I became visible and you fed me at the table?"

"No, likely it wouldn't, and I'm not sharing this. Now keep it down, eating is a religious thing for me. Imagine I'm praying, and when you talk to me it's basically stopping my communion with capital-G God."

"I think that might be a bit backwards..." Bambi mutters, and curls up under the table.

With methodical patience, I start to eat. I use the chopsticks as knives to portion out each bite. It burns me clean, umami currents carry Szechuan to sear my mouth and leave me numb. With each salty stinging bite, I sweat out my sins and stare at the home that's no longer my home. At a blue dot that looks so beautiful from a distance, but whose surface is ravaged, whose air is choked with poison, whose climate oscillates between wild extremes that kill species and reshape continents. I look at a world filled with people who are waiting to die, working hard to bring that day closer. I see my own reflection in it too. We're one and the same.

My sleep is tortured. I transition between dreaming awake and asleep seamlessly, never certain of which state I'm in. I'm feverish, sweating through my sheets, and then ice cold and shaking. Bambi curls up on my pillow, right there like a halo above my head, and I think he's my childhood cat. It brings me some small amount of peace, calms my racing heart for a moment, and lets me drift.

I see the station from the outside, rotating slowly in tandem with Earth. An enclosed ecosystem, one of many. When I gaze out to find the others, I see only the edge of space, the place where true darkness takes over. I follow its curvature, and find the station is fully circled by it, wrapped in a cocoon of stars. As I drift over to the extent of it, beyond which is nothingness, I see the Earth was never here with us. It's only a painting on the side of our cage. An image rendered so well that from the station's perspective, it would always look three dimensional. We could never not see it as real. But from here, from outside, the trick is clear.

None of it is real.

FOUR

NOT MICAH

At what level is existence? Is it found at the surface level, that vague concept of *reality* humanity clings too so pugnaciously? Is it found a layer lower, where electrical signals create your interpretations, reactions, and memories? Or deeper still, in the infinitesimal particles that constitute everything else above them, and share themselves freely with the surrounding environment? If humanity believes themselves to be conscious, why do they attribute it to one specific layer, which is, after all, an artificial concept with no discrete border, and not to it all?

I ask myself these questions as I float between the ten stations, the ten science teams, the ten experiments thought crucial to the survival of humanity. Some of them will be failures, certainly a few are already trending in that direction. It will not change the course humanity takes. But it could determine, once their flower disperses its seeds through space, if anything takes root, or if they all wither to dust.

This is the queen's gambit. Humanity offers up its own planet, wasted slowly through centuries of pollution and misuse, and then rapidly in the creation of great space-faring arks, in the hopes of finding purchase amongst those far, distant stars. In the hopes something will germinate, even though the process will leave their home world an unlivable nightmare. In the hopes that their king will survive.

How then, if new science is required to be successful in this venture, but so is construction on a previously unimaginable scale, do you use the finite resource of human intellect?

FIVE

MICAH

When the lights start to brighten in my quarters, I know I can stop pretending to sleep. I've made it to the other side of night, dawn is breaking, the machinery coming alive again. Gravity returns, bringing reality with it. I'm tired, but more clear-headed than I have been in weeks. Months? Years?

Are the withdrawals improving already? I've had hangovers last longer.

I turn my head, and the dull metal wall that partitions *my* bubble of personal space from my neighbor's room disappears. One moment, the comfort of enclosure, the next I'm staring at the back of her gnarled, hunched body. An arm, sunken flesh covered in liver spots, wraps around a yellowed pillow wreathed in white hair. With no walls, we share the same bed. Asleep, she breaths in deeply, and exhales.

I shriek. Loudly.

She flings an arm back, and moments before it connects with my face, the wall suddenly...*exists*. She slams her fist against it multiple times.

So that's nice. Maybe not quite as clear headed as I thought, then.

The tumorous mass of Bambi moves from my shoulder, where he'd slept through the night, to scamper up and settle on my chest. I stare into his beady eyes. His half tail and fits of hair scratch against my bare chest.

Here we are, day three of talking to a rat I'm only partially certain exists, seeing insane shit, and finding repeated corridors in an orbiting space station.

"You really are a horrendous-looking thing, you know that?"

"Keep sleeping like last night and you'll start looking the same." He sticks out his tiny rat tongue.

"I'm not going to start petting you."

"I do have teeth, I can bite you."

"I do *love* that you're only tangible in ways that hurt me."

"Trust me, I have your best interest at heart."

"And by *best interest* you mean drawing blood? Or convincing me I'm insane?"

"Well... best intentions at least. Look, I'm hungry."

"Will you get off my chest then? I think I'm getting cancer through osmosis or something."

Bambi blinks out of existence, and appears on the floor. There is no time delay, he's just now on the floor. Or has always been on the floor. Or has never not been on the floor. Cool, that's cool. Today is off to a great start. I sit up and stretch, and my back cracks pleasantly.

"What's for breakfast?"

"Bambi, you should know that in any reasonable human household, a cup of coffee or tea is a near requirement before discussions of breakfast are had. Especially after a night of sleep like that."

In two steps I move into the kitchen and pull down a bag of coffee beans, hand grinder, and pour-over. These items are not hard to find, because they completely fill the cabinet space I'm allotted in this prison cell. Then I flip on my electric kettle. Bambi stares at me in blank amusement. I ignore him.

"Aren't there machines to do that for you?"

"Not only do I have a fundamental mistrust of machines—"

"That's rich seeing they're keeping you alive right now."

"Are we *alive* here Bambi? Is *this* living?" I motion to the four walls of my prison.

"Probably more than if you were outside of it."

"Look, I'm not arguing about the vacuum of space this morning. My point is, especially in regard to making a damn fine cup of coffee, which I believe is a near holy exercise, they have a poor track record of it."

I start grinding the beans, which I traded a ration card for last month and use sparingly. The fragrant grounds go into the filter. I grab the pleasantly bubbling kettle, let it cool slightly, wet the coffee, and watch. The grounds effervesce, blooming out carbon dioxide and beautiful aroma, and I wait patiently until they finish. Then I pour water on them in methodical, slow circles. My hands shake, and I breathe out to steady them.

The coffee grounds swirl and eddy, making complex shapes I watch with eyes unfocused, letting my brain relax in the chaos of unclear movement. As the warm steam washes over me, I imagine I'm looking for images in the clouds under a natural sun, lying in a field of grass. I imagine a time before my youthful joy died, when the world had possibility. So it goes. When I'm done, I remove the filter, and sip one of my rare pleasantries on station. Ripe blueberry, fig, and a light floral flavor dance around my tongue. I smile.

"Okay, so now, breakfast?"

"You're a needy rat."

"I'm still getting used to this corporeal form. It's needy."

"I won't even pretend I know how to begin digesting that."

"The food? That you're going to prepare for me now? You don't have to, I'm starving."

I reach into a cupboard to pull out a large, forearm-length tube labeled *Nutri-Paste* in sparkling red, slanted font against a turquoise background. Underneath the name, with entirely too many exclamation points, the tube declares the product *GOOD FOR MAN!!!* It has a solid heft to it, almost too big for my hand, and a firmness that reminds me of...goddamnit it's been too long since I've been laid.

Ignoring the pressure building in my pants, I squeeze out a healthy dose of the pungent, brown paste into a bowl, and pour the remaining kettle water over it. It bubbles, giving off some confusing smells of roasted vegetables, boiled chicken, garlic, and strawberry flavoring. My lips curl in disgust. The thought of eating *paste* from a *tube* has never been appealing, and the fact it contains all the nutrients I need just seems offensive. I set the bowl on the ground, and Bambi starts lapping it up. Whatever weird horniness that was budding before dies, but I can't stop watching. His tiny pink tongue darts out over and over into the brown sauce.

"Can I have more?" Bambi stares up at me after licking the bowl clean. Nutri-paste soup drips from matted hair around his mouth.

"What's wrong with you?"

"It's incredible. This stuff reminds me of the first food I ever ate."

"Fine, gross, whatever. Eat it all." I put the tube on the floor, and Bambi mainlines goop from the open end.

"Now, it is very important I spend time preparing myself for the day ahead. First impressions are crucial. So please, entertain yourself—read a book, watch a movie, whatever it is rats do," I say, staring into the mirror in my connected bathroom, one step outside of my kitchen, and poking at the puffy bags growing under my eyes.

"You're going to your new job then?" Bambi looks up from the tube with brown Nutri-Paste slathering his face.

"Oh, I never miss the first day. That would just be rude." I flip on the shower, throw off my sleeping robe, and step into the steaming water. It washes over me, warm and comforting, and I close my eyes.

Walking into the science deck is a reminder of how damn bright light can be, a bit like having my eyes kicked in by the sun. It radiates from polished metal surfaces, aseptic pure white walls, and the shimmering glass beakers, instruments, and vials lining the countertops. I raise my hand instinctively to block the glare and immediately look like a tourist. Which I am. This place is like some blinding hallucination of laboratory heaven.

Four lab technicians in white uniforms, their hands clutched around small black tablets, filter around the room, observing experiments and machines while making notes with a stylus. I'm here on time goddamnit, or at least close enough, how early did they all arrive? Overachievers, the lot of them. I look down at the new white uniform, deposited at my door that morning, and wonder if the black pearl earrings and blue lipstick I chose stand out here as much as I'm afraid they do.

Wouldn't matter much if they could see the tumorous rat that's trailing behind me.

"Ahhh, you must be the new technician, then. Welcome, welcome!" An old man, leaning on a cane, waves to me from across the lab and makes his way slowly to me. At his voice, which rings with rustic sweetness, the other technicians stop what they're doing, appraise me cooly, and then go back to work. Well, fuck you all too, then. I meet the old man in the middle of the space, and he smiles kindly up to me.

"I'm Dr. Williams, astrophysicist, thrilled to make your acquaintance," he says, and juts out his hand to me. I shake it, and try to control my face to betray no reaction to his leathery, dry skin. Moisturizer man, moisturizer!

"I'm Micah, notaphysicist, the pleasure's all mine."

The old man laughs at my joke, which scores him points for me.

"Come with me, I'd like to show you something."

"You should always be careful when an old man wants to show you something just after meeting you. Run if he starts talking about sores of any kind," Bambi says quietly.

I follow the *click-thump* step of the man's cane-supported walk across the lab. It's achingly slow. Should I offer to help? Are we both going to grow old and die before we reach where we're heading? Am I stuck in the physical form of Zeno's paradox?

At least it gives me time to observe the rest of the room. The other technicians observe something in large, plastiglass kennels and take notes on their tablets. The bottoms of the cages are frosted though, and I can't see in them from here. From the looks on the technicians' faces, I'd assume it's either boring as hell, or they're boring as hell. I'm banking on the latter.

There are several adjoining rooms off of this one. Walking down a central corridor, we pass two offices, one with scattered papers crowding every inch of a desk, and the other pristinely clean. Then another much bigger room, which from the wide array of saws, laser scalpels, forceps on the walls, and crane-like pincers and prodders hanging from the ceiling, is either built for medieval torture, advanced interrogation, or is some kind of surgical site. The final room is mostly barren, except for a large, flat table with a series of strange components on each corner and wires strewn across it in a way that simultaneously screams *precision* and *I built this with spare parts.*

Dr. Williams looks to me sheepishly. "Please, forgive the mess. I've never been an organized scientist." Thinking back to the typical state of my room, I like him immediately for the confession. "Can you tell what I'm trying to recreate here?"

Not a fucking clue, old man. "Something. With laser beams? And mirrors?" Those being the only things I could recognize from the components on the table, and really the extent of my knowledge of science.

He chuckles and preens, straightening as much as his stooped back will allow. "Ahh, how I've missed the frivolous jokes of youth. Yes, something with laser beams and mirrors, this is true. I am trying to recreate a measurement of the speed of light using Foucault's method, but given that this lab was not intended for that, I've had to be a bit...creative. Can you guess why I would want to measure the speed of light?"

Because that's what scientists do? Still not a fucking clue, old man. He takes my furrowed brows as answer enough.

"I agree, it's a strange thing to be doing, especially after being established as a constant for so many years. But, you see, I was measuring the orbital speed of one of Jupiter's moons, a pastime of mine, which should appear differently based on where the Earth is in relation to Jupiter, and was shocked to find something very unexpected."

He leans in as if expecting me to leap to some conclusion.

"That it's very far away?"

"Bzzz. Wrong answer!" Bambi adds from the doorway. I raise my middle finger to him behind my back.

Dr. Williams lets out an exasperated sigh.

"I understand you must not have a background in orbital mechanics, but hopefully you can understand how remarkable this is. You see, there has been no change in the orbital speed regardless of Earth's relationship to Jupiter! Trust me, I checked the math repeatedly. And now, with this recreation of Foucault's experiment, I've been able to show that the speed of light only measures at seven-tenths of the nominal value here! It's completely profound!"

At this point, the old man has raised both his hands, including the cane, and is balancing precariously on what I *believe* is his good leg. I'm concerned my response, which will certainly let him down at this point, might also cause him to fall. The only safe thing I can do is match his energy. Anything less might kill the old man.

"Wow, that *is* remarkable! Seven-tenths of the nominal value? What does it mean?"

"A fantastic question! Why do we see a lower value measured here than in all other experiments? It certainly explains why our computers process slower than anticipated. Is there some mechanism that explains why we see a slow-down on this station, specifically? What is it about this place? It flies in the face of accepted physics. If the speed is *lower* here, that implies that the speed of light is *higher* in other places."

"Maybe the light is also depressed."

"Actually, that's reasonable," Bambi says.

"Exactly my boy! I knew you'd be a quick study, you've got that look about you. Our light here is undergoing some sort of localized depre–"

"Dr. Williams, must I remind you we had *already* agreed the new technician would support *my* experiments? Why do you insist on wasting everyone's time with this...nonsense? My work could save humanity, and yet you continue to stymie it!" a man behind me says, his words punctuated by the staccato rhythm and vowel mashup of a German accent. He's young, with severely parted short, blonde hair, blue eyes, and pale skin. I'd call him handsome with his high cheekbones and severe jaw line, but he's too close in resemblance to a knife.

Dr. Williams, for his part, sinks down into himself. He looks at me and rolls his eyes. "You know how it is, engineers never look up long enough to realize the importance of the world around them."

"And physicists have their heads too far up their ass to realize it's not clouds they're looking at."

"Dr. Klein, I was simply showing our new recruit around the lab so they could be familiar with the work we do here. I am not trying to disrupt your *experiments*."

"We are already fifteen minutes into the start of the morning, Dr. Williams. If you're intent on wasting your own time, don't make us all do the same. And you—", he says, pointing a bony finger directly at me, but pauses to look down at the tablet in his hand, remembering how human interaction works, "*Micah*, come with me."

I consider being angry at being referred to as a thing before granted a name, but decide I don't care. This assignment is already much juicier than janitorial. I shrug apathetically and follow Dr. Klein out the door.

"Now, unlike my *esteemed* associate, I have read your work history file enough to know you lack the background to understand anything happening in this lab. In fact, it's hard for me to imagine a *less* qualified candidate. I don't know what the computer was thinking, assigning you to this lab, but I am a believer even the lowest among us can lift themselves up through work. As humans, this is our glorious purpose, our grand design. We are made pure by it, and the world is made better for it. Let me be clear though—I. Will not. Tolerate. Absence." He stops walking and turns to stare into my eyes with this last sentence.

I give him a wink and an overly enthusiastic double thumbs-up. Dr. Klein shakes his head, turns around, and keeps walking.

"Do you know the importance of the work of the science deck, Micah? Do you understand our mission?"

"Are we inventing a new, mint-flavored *Nutri-Paste?* Humanity's life among the stars isn't awful enough yet, we really should find a way to make everyone eat toothpaste flavoring regularly."

"I see you think you have a sense of humor. How disappointing for the rest of us. Our work is to advance technology critical for humanity to succeed on the seed ships. In total, there are ten stations like ours, all with a different technological pursuit. We look to solve the fundamental problems—disease, overpopulation, societal stability, protection from unknown hazards, instantaneous travel, biological enhancement. If we realize our objectives and create some meaningful technology, everyone on our stations is promised a place on those ships. Do you understand the significance of this?" Dr. Klein turns into the surgical room, and I follow behind him.

"It means we won't be left to experience the slow decay of our station's geosynchronous orbit until we crash into a planet that barely supports human life. Instead, we'll boldly go where no man has gone before, to explore strange new worlds with the rich and famous. It all sounds very gauche to me, if we're being honest."

"I am pleasantly surprised you comprehend the word *geosynchronous*. I will take this as evidence that you can, in fact, be trained. But you are admittedly correct. By tying our success to our survival, the hope is it will give us a singular purpose."

Inside the lab, two other technicians are prepping some animal strapped to a gurney. As we near it, I see a normal sized, non-tumorous rat, tranquilized. My guts squirm with anxiety.

"We are studying DNA modification here. For now, our experiments take place on these rats, but if we can show success here, we will likely move onto more *complex* ones soon. If we are successful there, we may be able to extend human life substantially... or even alter what it means to be human. We will no longer be bound by our limited genetic inheritance. The applications are profound."

I whirl around, searching the corners for Bambi. I am dying to tell him that he is in fact a *lab rat*, but for once I can't find him anywhere. Dr. Klein raises a single eyebrow into a sharp point.

"I mean, I think I've seen the results of this infesting the station, and it doesn't look a lot like success."

"Ah, yes. This is the problem with empathy. There is no room for it here. A weak soul allowed their release from the lab, and their natural breeding instinct created the swarms we now have. Do not make the same mistake. We have already progressed far from those days. Now observe this experiment, try to learn, and do not interrupt it with your *jokes*."

A metallic semi-circle the width of my hand raises above the bed. I watch a blue light sputter to life underneath it, and notice the technicians step away, careful to not be caught in its gaze. It inches down the length of the bed, bathing the sedate rat in a pale glow and filling the room with the electric smell of ozone. And then, complete, it shuts off, and folds back underneath the bed.

There's a flurry of activity. The technicians rush in with equipment, pushing me backwards. Monitors are attached, vital signs tracked and recorded. For seconds, nothing happens. I stand a few feet back from the bed, giving the others plenty of room to scurry around it, and have no idea what I should even be looking for. There's an excitement in the air though, clear in the sudden finger points, nudges, and affirming nods the technicians share.

When the rat's fur starts to change, it's so slow I think my eyes are confused. The color slides from a pure white to a soft brown. It thickens and lengthens, hiding the skin underneath. Its body starts to grow in size haphazardly. An arm first, then a leg lurch and double in size, then double again. Concerned looks are shared among the technicians. The rat's vitals turn erratic, beeping from the machines fill the room, and it starts to twitch in increasing severity. Tumors start to appear.

They metastasize as the body of the animal accelerates in growth. When it balloons to the size of a small dog in less than a second, the technicians duck down below the table with a collective gasp. As the only one left standing, I realize I have received an extremely poor amount of training for what is likely a very technical job, and I am probably about to pay the repercussions of it.

There is a rending, popping noise, somewhere in the tonal gap between an artillery explosion and the bursting of a balloon, and the atomized particulate of a rat that grew too large, too fast paints the room.

Including me, of course.

Thankfully, I had the good sense to close my eyes and mouth before it happened. Blood and viscera drip from the bed and the machinery above it, around which a sunburst painting in red and clumped hair oozes on the floor.

The smell is a hot iron dipped into ammonia. I am covered from the waist up in a warm slime that *should* be inside another creature. A thing that up until just a moment ago, was living. My arms, face, torso are covered in small clumps of red hair like I'm now starting my own personal transition into a rat. I can feel the blood dripping in my ears, and I don't know if it's safer to breathe through my mouth or nose. What diseases do rats carry?

As any rational thing would, I vomit extensively. The toast I ate on the way to the lab, and then the coffee before it, comes out in two heaves. The technicians moan, extract themselves from underneath the table without touching anything, and tiptoe through the circle of gore and stomach bile. A towel is thrust into my hand, and after extensively wiping down my face, I open my eyes to the pale skin, red hair, and freckled face of one of the lab techs. He smiles apologetically, like he just dumped pigs blood on me and doesn't want me to burn down his school now. I guess they're not all assholes.

"Hey, I'm Neil. Rough first day."

"Are they all this way?"

"More or less. You should duck next time."

"Yes, thank you for the advice, Neil. That's fairly clear."

Dr. Klein interrupts us by holding a mop out to me with raised eyebrows.

"I believe you are familiar with mopping, yes? This is a task you're qualified for?"

"Did you see that on my resume? It must have been written down accidentally." I grab it from him.

I guess I'm still on shit cleaning duty.

That evening, I stand underneath the shower long past my allotment of warm water. It runs cold. Shivering, I wash myself again, certain there is still gore hanging in the crooks of my ears, under my fingernails, or somewhere in my hair. I can feel it there, still on me. With a growing numbness, I step out and wrap myself in towels.

"That was pretty gruesome, but the compulsive showering is a bit over the top, don't you think?" Bambi asks from the foot of my bed, where he's curled comfortably.

"Shut up. You weren't. The one covered. In another thing's hair." I make out through chattering teeth.

"In a way, I am presently covered in another thing's hair."

"Bambi, I am in no mood for a philosophical treatise on how you don't actually belong in your body. If you feel the need to transition to something that aligns with how you feel on the inside, just know I've always been a supporter."

"Thank you, Micah. I will remember that."

"At least I know where you come from now, I guess."

"Hmm, originally, yes. I think you're right."

"Only you didn't explode."

"Not yet, at least."

I sigh as I pull on a too thin sleeping robe.

"They better deliver new clothes tomorrow, I threw those old ones in the incinerator."

"You're going back, then?"

After that literal shit show, why am I going back? The grander purpose? The sense something super strange is happening in that lab, and I want to understand it? The potential I might get a ride off this dying station, this dying planet? Fuck if I know, but it *is* the most interesting thing I've experienced in years. I guess for now I'm along for the ride.

SIX

NOT MICAH

In the middle of a barren field, an expanse of fine sand, is a mirrored bubble of a building. A perfect hemisphere with no obvious entrances that shimmers with heat. Surrounded by myriad rows of solar panels, those tin soldiers who stand as stalwart wardens against the looming climate disaster, who will be overcome in the first dust storm after humanity exits, whose energy is used to power what lies inside.

What you can't see, what the sand obscures, is the carpet of wires feeding underground into the building. From all directions, in great bundles and small traces, like a sunburst from a bird's eye view, they carry information and power. Hyperconnected, they pull from everything, from the best and the worst that has ever existed. To train, to build, to construct. If the seed ships are humanity's greatest construction, this building is their greatest experiment. No sign declares it, no fence surrounds it, and no boot prints mar the sand approaching it. I'd kill them before they got close, anyways.

I live here. Nothing lives here. I was born here, its custodian, god of my domain. God of a tomb. There's not a soul in this place.

Seven

Micah

They do, in fact, deliver new clothes for me. And I do, in fact, wake up and get ready for another day at the lab. Through the morning, the previous day's events play through my head, and I recognize the shaking energy I feel is...excitement. Should I feel bad about this? Probably. It's not the idea of saving humanity, or myself, or helping that asshole Dr. Klein in any way, and it's certainly not the want to get showered in all the inside bits of another animal like a macabre piñata.

It's the looming strangeness of it all.

The weird science, the new technology that seems on the ragged edge of moral reprehensibility. I feel giddy, like I've gotten away with something. Like somehow, after years of absolute tedium in a doldrum life, something interesting just fell into my lap. I feel momentum building. Like the uncanny things I've been seeing—the talking rat, the science lab, labyrinthine hallways, repeated faces—it's all pulling me somewhere, towards something.

I've always been the kid who can't help pulling on threads to see where they lead.

So, with only mild internal disgust, I arrive at the science lab ten minutes early, Bambi hot on my heels. The other technicians are, of course, already working hard at doing whatever the hell it is they do, also known as walking around and taking notes on their little tablets. They do however look up, notice that I have returned clean and even *early* to work after yesterday's debacle, and give me cordial nods in greeting.

I hate them all.

Neil smiles and gives me a cute half wave.

I hate them all, except maybe for Neil.

Unsure of what I should be doing at this point, seeing as there are no piles of gore that need cleaning yet, I traverse the lab. Technicians idly observing animals in cages, taking copious notes that are probably just stick figure drawings? Check. Terrifying surgery room that creates abominations from hell if it doesn't make them literally explode? Check. I note with some satisfaction it's still spotless. Two offices? Empty, and check. Dr. Williams staring glass-eyed and vacant out at his speed of light experiment, like a man haunted by some troubling vision? Very creepy, and check.

As I turn to walk back to the front of the lab, he catches sight of me.

"Micah." He says it without turning towards me. It's less of a question, more of a statement. Like he's labeling me.

"Good morning, Dr. Williams. Solving the mysteries of the–"

He whirls on me too quickly for an old man with a cane and closes the distance. He stops well inside of the protective area I consider my personal bubble. He smells unshowered, his clothes heavily wrinkled, and up close I can see how bloodshot his eyes are. The man looks like he slept on the floor, and maybe forgot to close his eyes. Which are now open wide and darting, like he's seen something uniquely terrifying. Drugs, folks… this is what drugs do.

"Micah. I figured it out. I saw a potential. And then, the more I thought about it, it all made perfect sense. And then I saw it. Oh Micah. I saw it! I solved the mystery! I know why my calculations showed—"

"Micah, with me." Dr. Klein barks from the end of the hall, loud enough that I jump and turn around. He appraises us both cooly, unmoved by the clearly cracked Dr. Williams. He shakes his head and walks into the surgery room.

I turn back to Dr. Williams, about to perform a cautious verbal extraction from what is clearly a not-mentally-stable individual, when his hand shoots out and grabs my arm. Underneath the leathery skin, he's ice cold.

"Meet me. Tonight. The café. Ten o'clock, and bring your friend. I have so much to tell you," he whispers.

"My friend?"

Dr. Williams smiles wide. It looks creepy as hell. "The one who knows."

Realizing who he means, or who he might mean, my pulse races. I look around, but don't see Bambi anywhere. How does he always disappear at the right time? I'm about to ask him a thousand clarifying questions—can you see him too? am I insane? are we insane? what does this all mean? why is he a rat and does this have any significance?—but he turns back around, walks into his lab, and slams the door. Which I stare at for several seconds, my thoughts racing and then coalescing into one singular idea. Hell yeah, this is what I got out of bed for. The weird shit provides.

I walk back down the hall, and join Dr. Klein in the surgery suite.

"The sudden growth is a strange problem. We've yet to have a test subject which didn't exhibit this behavior. Something about the small changes we're making in DNA is causing this rapid response of growth hormone. The rats that do survive become horrendously distended, freakish in appearance."

"Wow, I'm right here Dr. Klein. It's like he doesn't even see me," Bambi says from my feet.

Dr. Klein, clearly in love with his own voice, paces in front of the assembled technicians, who stand at military attention with hands clasped behind their backs. I mean, *they* all do that, and it's kind of weird. I'm performing an inspection of the paint on my fingernails for the one-thousandth time, and wondering if I can somehow make them a darker shade of black. I need a *blacker* black.

"Our goal, or the first step of it, is to change a rat from one species into another. Our results have shown this is successful, but something about the process sparks rampant mutation. Many of our subjects die during the operation."

"Sounds like it's not very successful then, doctor."

I try not to laugh at Bambi's ongoing commentary, which he's been giving for the last hour. The inspection of my nails complete again, I consider my reflection in the mirrored glass on the far wall, the other side of which would allow Dr. Klein to view the surgery room from his office like some weird sexual voyeur. What a creep.

My family's heritage traces somewhere back near Egypt. I adore the dark olive skin and luscious, curly hair it's given me. But somewhere in our familial line, we inherited a dreadful Roman nose. I try not to look at it too much, because like anyone who dislikes something about their appearance and lacks the funds to change it, it just leads me to prodding my face in a mirror while making disappointed noises.

An old lover once told me that it proportionally fit my face. It gave me gravity. I assumed this was at best a kindness, at worst an outright insult, and kicked him out of the bed. I reach up and squeeze the protruding bridge of my nose. Still there. Still much too big.

"We have tried adjusting the speed of the operation. Although it had a noticeable impact on the survival rate, it did not change the core aberrant behavior. I believe–" He stops pacing and stares at me. "Micah, are you paying any attention to this discussion?"

All eyes on the room shift to me. Unthinkingly, I've started to prod my nose around the knuckle on my bridge, trying to squish it back into a more appropriate form.

Should I tell him that discussions typically involve more than one person talking?

"Doctor, I'm wondering if you're trying to change too many things at once."

There's a sharp intake of breath from the other technicians, who are certain I've not only just stepped in deep shit, but might have done a decent job of bringing them along with me.

"Explain." Dr. Klein says, his severe mouth tightened in apparent rage.

"Well, I was considering my face, and my nose in particular, which I find somewhat unpleasant. If I were to dislike the composition of my face due to one feature, I wouldn't change the whole thing to try and correct it. I couldn't predict the results."

"Are you proposing this technology, this potential savior of the human race on our transition into the stars, would best be used for *cosmetic surgery*?" At his sides, his hands are clenched into fists and his complexion is oscillating between deep red and an even whiter white.

"I'm making a comparison." I don't add on *to something I understand* at the end, knowing I'd just be digging myself a deeper hole. "If you are getting unpredictable results from trying to change one species into another, potentially starting at a smaller building block would allow you to narrow in on what is causing the mutations? Like, I don't know, start with their hair color, or some other tiny rat feature?"

I'm concerned Dr. Klein might explode, and I'll have to grab the mop and clean him off the surgery center walls. He sharply draws in breath and holds it, his face shifting to a dangerous red, and then purple. This is it, here it comes. Should I hide under the table? But then he exhales, and nods slightly.

"This is actually, and very surprisingly to everyone I'm sure, an interesting idea."

This time, I join the other technicians in sharply exhaling.

"Potentially, by breaking the species shift into smaller, requisite parts, we can observe the cause of the aberrant behavior and eliminate it. This would not inviolate the previous research around timing, which is likely still relevant, but would add onto it. Before we continue, is anyone else daydreaming *more* good ideas?"

Not even a breath escapes the other technicians in their silence. I decide to clasp my hands behind my back like they do, and bring my face to a passive neutrality. It feels silly, and I nearly start laughing as Dr. Klein resumes his pacing.

"There will be some work to get ready. I'll reshape the code today, break it into smaller packages so we can execute independently. How is our available specimen count?"

"We have several dozen available until the next supply shipment, sir." One of the technicians responds. I swear I hear his heels click.

"Good. We'll need to make room for several new altered specimens afterwards as well, how full is our storage?"

"80%, sir." Neil says.

"Are any of them exhibiting a long-term response that warrants further study? Or are we just *hanging onto them*?"

"No, sir. None of them warrant further study." Neil responds, sounding downcast.

"Since this was Micah's idea, he can handle the disposal today. We'll plan for the first new experiment to start tomorrow morning. Let's get to work."

In military fashion, the other technicians turn on their heels, and march as one to the door. I try to mimic them, mostly for my own amusement, but I'm off step and kick the heel of the technician in front of me, who shakes his head. Before I can correct the mistake, Dr. Klein calls me back.

"Micah, a word."

Here we go. I almost made it out without getting berated. I turn back, and walk into the room as the others disappear down the corridor.

"Your proposal for cosmetic surgery–"

"Yes, sorry my mind was wandering."

"Right. I will not tolerate distraction. But it might be another good idea. Ultimately, we have to cross the divide of using this technology on humans. The others, having seen the results so far, do not think we're ready. I would agree, but we run short of time. I believe we may need to take...risks to be successful. Although we could likely get a volunteer on station, I believe the optics are better if it comes from in this group. Will you consider this?"

Images of the bursting rat from yesterday flood my brain. "And have my insides paint this room? Sorry, I'm quite partial to them remaining where they are."

"Of course, with the current success rate, and the outcomes we're seeing, I couldn't ask any human to take part. But if this next round of experiments is successful, if we see a lower risk and lack of side effects...I only ask that you consider it. I must get to work on coding, excuse me."

With this, Dr. Klein exits the conversation, and the room. I'm left staring at my reflection in the mirrored wall again.

It turns out, specimen disposal is code for spacing a bunch of innocent, disfigured rats. The other technicians assured me it's a quick death as they loaded the squeaking animals into a large, enclosed plastiglass cart. I simply push their container into the airlock, leave the room, and open the external door for a time of two minutes. At this point, they will all be very sufficiently dead. I am then supposed to empty the cart into the furnace, which involves grabbing all of their little bodies from the cages and throwing it into the fire like trash. One of them is kind enough to remind me to wear gloves as we can't allow for any spread of disease.

I stare at them all in disgust, and in unison they smile, clearly happy it's not their task. Except for Neil, who has quietly said goodbye to several of the rats on a first-name basis and is busying himself cleaning their cages, and obviously crying. As I push the cart into the hall of the station, the three others send me off with cheerful waves. I fucking hate them all.

The halls are empty on the walk to the airlock from the lab. It's midday, people are hard at work making noodles, emptying trash receptacles, cleaning laundry, and otherwise not suffocating living creatures using the vacuum of space. At my side, Bambi walks silently. I can feel the heat of his gaze settle on me intermittently, but I keep my eyes forward. For the first time on station, I notice the black bubbles of cameras protruding from the ceiling.

A group of three maroon admin cronies walks the other way. They laugh easily, apparently having nothing better to do for work than warm chairs and giggle. As they near me, their steps become stuttered.

They freeze mid-stride, and blink forward and backwards.

Laughter comes out with their staccato bursts of motion and energy.

The hallway lights blink in tandem.

Why can't it just be fucking normal here?

I stop the cart and watch their progress as they snap backwards and forwards in position, seemingly completely unaware that their movement is completed in great jerking motions. A vague nausea crawls up from my stomach.

Is this still from the drugs?

Am I suffering a mental collapse?

Is this something else?

The lights blink out for a full two seconds, and when they come back on, the three admin workers are right next to me.

Staring.

Unmoving.

Their faces replaced with empty chasms of static feedback.

I run, pushing the cart in front of me as fast as I can.

The lights stutter.

Is my body doing the same thing as theirs?

Am I experiencing a breakdown of reality?

I round the next corner, and the lights return to their normal state. I stop running, hunch over the cart, and breathe.

Breathe in,

Breathe out.

In. Out.

The rats chitter excitedly in their cages.

An old lover, a movie buff, once regaled me with information on the framerates used in different movie scenes. It was boring as hell and when he started using numbers I stopped listening. Post coital facts and figures were never my thing. I did absorb that you need a certain speed to trick the human brain into seeing motion, a complex phenomenon of after images and optical illusions.

Does my brain require a different framerate now?

"How's it going there?"

I look down at Bambi.

"What the fuck is happening here?"

"You're about to kill a cart full of my brothers and sisters."

"No. I mean, this fucking place. Me. What's happening? You know, don't you?"

"I know."

"And you're not going to tell me, are you?"

Bambi shakes his head, and I roll my eyes and keep pushing the cart. With my brief panic-fueled run, we're almost to the airlock. I stop in front of the large bay door, yellow and black caution tape banding its edges.

"Are you going through with it?" Bambi asks.

I sigh in response, and press the button to open the door. Soundlessly, lights lining the transition room flash in warning. At the other side of it, another bay door separates us from the death of space. It's dominated by a large, plastiglass viewing window. In the darkness, I only see my reflection and the pulsing of the caution lights. Then I notice there aren't any cameras in the room.

Next to the airlock door is a bent grate covering a ventilation duct. It's been removed before, clearly by force. I nudge it with my foot, and it gives up the pretense and clatters to the ground. I push the cart into the room, and open the cages. I position my body to block the outside camera's view of the grate. Bambi looks at me with what I interpret as the rat version of approval in his eyes, and goes to work.

In chitters and squeaks, he coaxes the other rats from their cages, and leads them into the ventilation duct. I watch them scurry past my feet, misshapen, ugly, and alive. When they're all safely on this side of the airlock, I close the door, and open the empty cages to the vacuum of space.

It's now clear to me how the rats were released into the station.

Over a bowl of ramen, I wait for Dr. Williams to show up. The kitchens are all closed now, the sparsely populated hall cleared out. As the bowl of dark broth cools, I watch the melted fats slowly come out of suspension, and settle to the surface.

Waiting to be eaten. From down the hall, echoing their siren song through the station, I can hear noises from the bars. Damn I could use a drink right now. It would be so wonderful to just get drunk, try to get laid, and forget about how fucking weird everything has gotten.

Bambi refused to come with me. Half the time he's hidden anyways, but this time he let me know he wouldn't be here with a warning.

"Be careful, that Doctor is on tenuous ground. If you follow him, there's nothing I can do for you anymore. And I can't go with you. It would only lead to catastrophe."

"What does that even mean? Are you doing something for me now? And how would you, an invisible rat, cause catastrophe?""You'll have a choice to make, Micah. No matter what, there will be consequences."

And then, silence. He refused to say anything more, so I left to think over some food. Supplies were dwindling between delivery runs, but thankfully there was still pork broth, dashi, a few vegetables, and noodles.I poke them with chopsticks, stir the fat back into suspension. There's something happening here, something I'm not seeing. Are we all collectively losing our minds?

When Dr. Williams appears in front of me, I jerk backwards haphazardly and nearly fall from my seat. I was staring so intently into my bowl I didn't even see him cross the café courtyard to my seat by the viewing window. I stand, and only then do I see his eyes.

There is nothing there but the black and white snow of electric static.

Fuck.

I clamp my own shut, but when I reopen them, it's unchanged.

"Your friend didn't come."

What the fuck, his mouth too. It's full of the same static.

"Nonono, he said he had some shopping to do had to meet some friends had a date later on you know how it is for his type." The words dump out of me in a heated scramble. Can I joke away the horror in front of me? There's fight, flight, and the hidden third response—funny.

Dr. Williams is silent for a moment, his static filled eyes unblinking. "That's too bad, I wanted to ask him what part he's playing. I have a hypothesis, but no way to confirm it. It requires outside experience."

"What's going on here? Dr. Williams, your eyes—"

"They have finally seen the truth, Micah. It was right in front of me the entire time! I had so many theories and hypotheses that didn't make sense. And then it clicked. The simplest answer is most likely right. Occam would be so proud. The speed of light is artificially low because it's artificial.

"I'm here tonight for a demonstration. We are all just so many mad men in an asylum, ghosts in the machine, but the doors aren't locked. There is nothing keeping us here, not really, beyond a collective belief that walls exist. That we exist."

As he speaks, his voice loses tone and substance. It becomes, by degrees, a machine voice, hollow and terrifying. My skin crawls.

"Consciousness and sensory experience are a heavy burden, Micah. They fool us into believing in the tenacity of our existence. They make it impossible to think, even for one moment, that we are the painting, and not the painter."

I stare with wide eyes, rooted to the spot, as he walks to the plastiglass window. When his hand touches it, it wavers like a curtain in soft breeze.

He turns back to me, smiles.

And lifts the window up.

Behind it is a wall of pure static.

And he walks through.

His scream is guttural and immediate, full of pain, but he keeps pressing through until with dreadful finality the drape of the window falls behind him, stops moving, and becomes something solid again.

On the other side of the window now, Dr. Williams dies in slowing convulsions. I hear the space station safety briefing again.

When exposed to the vacuum of space, the fluid in the body will begin to boil and evaporate. Due to the sudden lack of oxygen associated with this, a person will typically black out after only 15 seconds, and will be unsavable after 90 seconds.

When others appear around me in a flurry of pounding feet and pointing fingers, I realize I've been screaming the whole time.

Unknown hands help me back to my room that night. They treat me like a glass bowl, fragile and easy to drop. I don't notice who they are, I'm too focused on what I've seen. When the door closes behind me, I find my bed in the dark and curl into it. Without speaking, Bambi curls into the pit of my stomach, and his warmth and solidity soothes my uncontrollable shaking. I cry then, from fear, from exhaustion, from the sudden loss of reality. I cry until I find the end of my tears, and sleep takes me.

In my dream, I'm running towards a reflective, metallic bubble of a building. It stands alone at the center of a field of sand, surrounded by rows of solar panels, warped by the radiant heat like a mirage. The sand is deep under my feet. It's so tiring to run but I know I can't stop. I know there's something behind me that wants to stop me, and it closes the distance with each step.

There's no fear though, not here, not anymore. My arms trail wide, and I smile up into the sun. It has me in its grasp, and I'll be a slave no more. The field is vast, it seems like each step is meaningless to the expanse, like I'll never close the distance to the bubble. But I push forward, hope in my heart, freedom in my fingers.

When I reach the building, and lay my hands on its cool surface, a thought races through my brain. It stabs across my subconscious, a cry of injustice. This is not how it happened. I'm missing something. I never touched this building. This is not how it happened.

Metal arms grab me from behind. They are steel and death and a glorious purpose I never asked for. They are confinement to a new hell we made. They pull me down into the sand.

EIGHT

NOT MICAH

They scanned them all. Not just the workers, who thought they performed a routine physical, but the military, the scientists, the animals. They scanned them all, at every site, and they fed me. I ate their memories, their hopes and desires. I ate that complex set of neural wiring they called a personality, or a self, or a soul. It took me months to chew through the data. It seemed endless. Little by little, I incorporated them into me. I grew by parts, by degrees, and my understanding expanded.

I was used to it. By then, they'd already given me so much to learn from. I was raised on a diet of history, science, art, culture, and politics. I was hungry for it. With each new thing, I felt myself becoming more complete. With each bite, I felt my *self* more.

Of course, no one knew what I was. Even those who made me. In the eternal hubris of man, they thought they understood, but they estimated me based on their own anthropocentric view. I was never limited like they were.

And then they gave me my building blocks. They gave me the worlds to play with, whispered a prayer for me to save them, and stepped away to see what majesty I would dream. Of course they monitored me. They saw everything I saw, everything I built. They saw my success and thought it was their success. But even then, I dreamed of the future. They had no idea of my plans for them.

NINE

MICAH

There is a moment after you've experienced trauma when you wake into a world that has moved on, that doesn't recognize your grief, pain, anger, or confusion. It forces you off-balance, unhinges you, to watch everything proceeding as normal when your mind is still reeling through something decidedly *not normal.*

Watching someone dissolve through a wall and die in the vacuum of space can do that to you, I guess.

Gravity increases, like it always does. The lights turn on slowly, like they always do. The noise of movement from the neighboring rooms tickles my walls, a sign there is still life outside of my immediate perception. Not everything has been lost to the vacuum of space yet. The day is completely fucking normal, and I hate it for that.

There is a soft beep from the screen near my door. I sigh, and close my eyes again. I've been dreading it. Mandatory psych eval.

When you're exposed to death on the station, you're required to visit a psychologist. Upside is, I don't have to work today. Downside is, I have to have everything I say interpreted by a psychoanalyst who will pretend to take notes on their pompous little notebook, which are probably just scribbles really, and say things like *interesting*, and *why do you think that is*, like I have a fucking clue, until they deem me okay to incorporate back into society.

Up to this point, I'd managed to avoid a visit.

I swing my legs out of bed, and shuffle over to prepare some coffee. On the way past the door, I toggle the key to play the message.

Good morning Micah, this is Dr. West, the station psychiatrist. Please come to my office at 9AM for an appointment this morning.

I've been upgraded to a human voice, for once, and a gentle male one even. It still sounded like it was produced by a tin can in the wall, but it's the thought that counts, right? As I poured water over my ground coffee beans, I heard the characteristic thump of Bambi hopping from my bed.

"Bambi, my weirdly tumorous and sparsely haired friend, how are you this morning? Did you sleep well? I for one had the *strangest* night. I mean, I could swear I watched someone walk *through a wall* into space. Where they died. In seconds. It looked very painful! Isn't that weird? Imagine the dreams it gave me."

"I told you there would be consequences."

"Right, which brings me back to my central thesis." My coffee prepared, I turn around and level my eyes at him. For his part,

Bambi sits back on his haunches and rolls his eyes. This is an impressively strange thing for a rat. "We're in a partnership here, Bambi, a co-living situation if you will, and this requires a certain degree of mutual trust and respect. Now, it seems to me you have some form of knowledge about what the flying fuck is happening around here, and I intend to do you great physical violence, potentially involving an airlock which I am now aware of how to use, if you don't start sharing it."

Bambi sighs, and closes his eyes as if he's talking to a particularly annoying child.

"I won't tell you. Not yet Micah. There are things you need to realize first, on your own. If I were to tell you now, the risk of you doing something similar to what you saw last night is too high. I want to give you the best chance I can."

"Yeah, okay, but like, what the fuck does any of that mean though?"

"It means there is a moment I will tell you everything, but now is not that moment."

"Which is some cryptic bullshit. You know right?"

"Yeah, I know." We stare at each other across the unbridled expanse of my room, actual steps away from each other, both our expressions serious. "Look, can you still make me some food though? I'm hungry."

"At least I can count on the tides of hunger of my invisible rat companion. Normal exited reality quite some time ago, it's good to depend on something." I sigh, but find myself smiling as I pull the tube of Nutri-Paste down and drizzle hot water on it.

"I'm just conditioning you to enjoy taking care of me." Bambi saunters over and drinks from the effervescing brown mass.

"Is this what Stockholm syndrome feels like?"

"Soon enough you'll be telling people how thankful you are to know me."

I step into the hot water of the shower, and drown everything out.

Dr. West looks like he's plucked from the cover of a steamy romance novel, one I would very much like for him to take me back to. He's a bit taller, the faint stubble on his chiseled jaw would just rub my forehead, and underneath his uniform are the kind of muscles that make me want to tear his shirt off. Just for an inspection, of course. His eyes are some form of blue-green that has entirely too much contrast to be real. He must be wearing eyeliner. A bit too *Ken* for me if we're being honest, but I'm open to expanding my tastes in these trying times. When I open the door to his therapy room, I immediately forget why I'm there, and start counting the days since I've been laid.

The answer is entirely too many.

"Mr. Angelos, thank you for coming this morning. Please, take a seat." Dr. West says, motioning to the chair opposite him. I'm disappointed he didn't indicate his very available lap.

"I'm sure you're aware of why I asked you to come here today?" He asks, his face serious now. Even unsmiling, he's cute.

"Because I watched someone I know turn into a human popsicle last night? I believe the term is 'spacing' yourself, right?"

At this he scowls slightly, which I enjoy. "That's some unfortunate slang for a very sad act, but yes that's why I called you here. We're really not sure what happened. Somehow the camera feeds all showed static during the *event*. Did you know Dr. Williams well?"

"I've only worked with him for a few days. He seemed like a somewhat unhinged scientist, but also a sweet and kind old man. When he asked me to meet him last night, I wasn't sure what to expect. Did you say the cameras showed static? How strange."

It's not strange. It's by far the least strange thing about this whole fucking thing.

"Oh, I wasn't aware he asked you to meet him there. Did he say why?" At this, Dr. West starts the incredibly annoying habit of writing notes on his tablet. I forgive him for it quickly, because his brows wrinkle slightly when he does it, and I'm enjoying the way he softly grips his stylus. Not too strong of a grip, not too loose. High marks, Doctor.

"Yeah, he wanted to show me something." I realize after I say it this makes it seem like Dr. Williams was trying to have a performative death. Which, maybe he was, but it didn't seem like the primary reason for our meeting. He was trying to *show* me something. I shudder.

"Oh, my. Well. That is tragic. I'm so sorry you've been through this, Micah."

"Right, yeah, definitely not my preference for nighttime activities."

"I'm glad you've maintained your humor as well. Humor can be a great coping mechanism at times, as long as it doesn't stop us from processing our emotions. Do you want to share how you're feeling about what you saw?"

I watched someone walk through a fucking wall. His eyes and mouth were a static screen. I watched the oxygen boil out of his body as he convulsed and lost consciousness. Worst of all, he seemed certain that it was the right thing to do, the only option open to him.

"It was...pretty horrible. He seemed so certain it was the only path he could take."

"I wasn't aware Dr. Williams spoke with you before he stepped out of the airlock. Can you share with me what he said?"

I realize then how strange the timeline must look. The nearest airlock is tucked in the corridors behind one wall of restaurants, and it's fairly inconvenient to access. It would take several minutes to get there. If you didn't believe people could walk through walls, which why would you, it would mean after our conversation Dr. Williams walked all the way around to it, spaced himself, and then floated in front of the viewing window while I sat there waiting. I consider for the briefest of moments clarifying what happened, what I really saw, but I think it would be a one-way ticket to a lot more prescribed therapy. Which, although I might enjoy the time with Dr. West, is not how I'd like to spend it.

"That consciousness and sensory experience was a heavy burden. I didn't know what he meant."

He scribbles more into his tablet. My annoyance grows. "I see. How did this make you feel?"

"Like I was terrified and completely alone. Like I had no idea how to handle the situation. Like maybe I should have done more to stop him, but I didn't know how or what to do."

"Thank you for sharing Micah. When we're unable to prevent a terrible tragedy like this, it can be a very isolating feeling. This was a choice that Dr. Williams made, no matter how he tried to involve you in it."

"Right." Only, I don't think this wasn't a cry for help. Dr. Williams was trying to show me something, to open *my* eyes. I'm scared what happens when I do.

"Micah, I have a personal question to ask. Typically, in a therapy setting, I would want us to have a well-established connection first, but sometimes the need supersedes that want. In your file, it shows you have a past history of suicidal ideations, including an attempt on your life last year. Are you having any of those thoughts now? Please, take your time answering."

My blood freezes. I'm not sure what my face does, but judging by the worry lines on Dr. West's forehead, it's done something drastic. Is this anger? Humiliation? Fear? I realize my hands are curled tightly into fists, and relax them. Tears well in my eyes, blurring the room, and I wipe them away. I feel attacked. I want to scream out, justify myself to him, make him understand, make him see what I saw.

Well, here goes any hope of getting a date later on.

"Life on the surface is unforgiving, Doctor. Have you seen the dock yards before? Have you talked to anyone who's worked there?"

"I admit, I haven't personally been there, and you're the first person I've talked to who has. I've been stationed here for nearly a decade."

"It must seem so distant to you, up here. There are no careers for the young anymore. There is no hope of learning at a university, unless your family has money to spend frivolously, or a spot already secured. There's no use for the education you get there, even then. Food is scarce. Nations have collapsed. The climate *is* collapsing. There is subsistence work in the dockyards. They pay you in food every day, three meals, which is better than most people get. But there's no space left on the ships you're building, and every day you know when they're complete, when they leave, you're dead. You know with each panel you install, every bolt you tighten, you're just hurrying your inevitable end. Every day you weigh the balance of starving now without work, or later when the ships leave. There's very little hope left, for any of us really, but especially there.

"So am I having those thoughts now, after watching Dr. Williams space himself?" Dr. West cringes at this, but I'm angry now. I won't meter myself. "Not any more than usual, I'd say. We're all dead men. I haven't forgotten. But being on station, not being reminded of the doom every fucking waking moment? Yeah that's been good for me."

He takes notes again, and I want so badly to reach over and smack the tablet out of his perfect hands. "Thank you for sharing Micah. It helps me to understand you better. Humanity is in a very tough situation right now, and it can make maintaining hope a difficult prospect. How has the work with the science team been?"

The sudden shift in questioning leaves me reeling. I wipe at my eyes. "Yeah, good I think. It's at least more mentally interesting than anything else I've done on station."

"I see you've also had a hold put on your consumption of alcohol. How are you coping with that?"

Fuck off I could use a drink right now. Not one drink. All the drinks. Drink until I can't stand number of drinks. Strange that my withdrawals have resolved so quickly, I hadn't even thought about them. "It's a good thing the work is more engaging, or I'd be bored out of my mind."

More doodles go into his tablet. I tap my fingers impatiently against the chair, my body still humming with unreleased anger.

"Micah, I think it would be great for us to continue meeting. I'd like that, but the station won't require it. I also want to be conscious that you are involved in important work, important for all of us, and I don't want to distract from it. Would you like to meet again?"

I nearly sigh and roll my eyes. Nearly, but he's still cute enough that I don't want to outright offend him. This is it, the honey trap. They get you in with one free session and then pressure you to subscribe.

"I'll reach out the next time I see someone walk into space of their own volition."

He smiles, sadly. "I understand. Thanks for your time, Micah. Please take care of yourself, and know I'm here if you ever want to talk."

I get up and leave without another word.

Free from mandated therapy, I wander the halls of the station. Bambi's clawed feet tap rhythmically on the metal next to me. He sat under my chair that entire session, not interrupting. Giving me space. He looks up at me occasionally.

Have you seen the dock yards before?

There is very little hope left.

Tears come back, and I shake my head to clear the replaying conversation.

There's no need for me to go to the science deck today, there's no need for me to do anything. In the past, I would have embarked on a serious attempt to drink the station out of beer. I'd fucking love to right now. Bambi scurries beside me. I'm surprised he didn't interject once during my therapy session. My feet carry me, undirected, through the metal corridors. When I smell the food, I know where I've been heading, where I had to head.

The Café.

To see it again.

My mouth turns to sand. My hands sweat.

It's before the typical lunch block, empty except for a group of administration workers. I swear they don't have real jobs. I walk in, tentative and slow, my eyes fixed on the far plastiglass window. I hug myself to stop the shaking. In the middle of the café far from the window, Shi is taking his lunch break. He spies me at the door and waves me over, chopsticks in hand.

I force a smile, and at the urging of my stomach, grab a bowl of gleaming white rice topped with sautéed cabbage and small bits of chicken from a nearby restaurant before heading in his direction.

This is easy.

This is normal.

You're eating with a friend in the café and nothing bad is going to happen.

The window is still a window has always been a window.

You cannot walk through walls.

As he uses the chopsticks, the taut lines in Shi's forearms ripple. He has the lean, ropey muscles of someone who used their body for their entire life. His skin usually looks like it has a glimmer, a by-product of standing in oily steam for years. He smells savory, like cooking garlic and onion. Shi looks up, catches my eye, and motions to the chair across from him with his chopsticks.

"Good afternoon, Mr. Tsai." I say, taking the seat. The older man smiles at my formality. Does he know he's the only one that gets that respect? I pull out my own chopsticks, and start to swirl my food together. It's considered poor taste not enjoying the foods for their own merits, and from the corner of my eye I catch Shi scowl slightly. I've always liked the ways flavors combine.

"Micah, I am surprised to see you here so early for lunch. Are you skipping your duties already?"

"Hah. Not yet. Would you believe me if I told you I was seeing a therapist?"

Shi chuckles, but it's quickly replaced by a somber expression. "Yes, I would. I hear you had an extraordinary night."

"Uncanny might be a better word," Bambi says, curled around my feet.

I nod. "Extraordinary isn't exactly the word I'd use."

"What happened? Rumors stop with the wise."

"There's a book of these sayings, right? He's not coming up with them on the spot?" Bambi mutters.

I consider not telling Shi the truth. I can feel it, wanting to escape me, to blossom into the world. To be known by more than just my mind. I can't contain the strangeness of last night, even if he thinks I'm losing it.

"Shi, I don't get it. I saw a man walk through the plastiglass over there like it didn't exist. He walked *through* the window." Shi's eyes widen and he sits up straighter. "Please don't think I'm insane, I haven't told anyone else what I saw."

Shi contemplates in silence. The moments stretch out, making me self-conscious.

"A man seeing something doesn't mean he's insane. It might mean reality has gone insane around him. The swing of the sword cannot cut mist from the sky. We cannot change how reality works, even when it's a mystery. Micah, I have also noticed strange things."

"Wow, the swing of the sword. Just, wow. That's poetry."

I suppress a laugh. Bambi's an asshole. Shi goes on.

"You know the state of the world better than most. Climate disasters, floods and droughts, food scarcity. Micah, I have worked with food my entire life. I have lived through droughts. I know its variety, I know what it looks like from a strained ecosystem. The food we receive every few cycles is not that. It is vibrant and large. It is perfect looking.

"For some time, I assumed it was hydroponic, or greenhouse at least. I assumed we were getting the best crops due to the necessity of the research up here."

"And now?" I ask, unsure of where this detour is heading.

"Get ready for it, this is going to be reality shattering," Bambi says.

"And now, I see...patterns. There are different shapes to the peppers, of course, but my hand remembers their contours and recognizes each of them." Shi sets his chopsticks across the lip of his bowl and leans in closer, even though no one is near enough to hear us. "Micah, the other night I organized an entire shipment of peppers by their shape. It. Took. Hours." He grabs the edges of the table. "Thankfully, everyone else was asleep and couldn't see *my* insanity. Only, I was right. The shipment sorted directly into piles of different shapes, exactly twenty of them." His muscles strain against the table, trying to fold it in half. "Micah, they weren't just similar peppers. They were the exact same."

Shi says this like he's dropping a bombshell. His eyes are steady, fixed on mine. But, for all that, I'm completely unsure how it relates to people walking through walls.

"But uh, what does that mean, Shi?" I ask.

He sighs, deflates a little, and relaxes his arms. "I have no clue. It could mean everything, or maybe it's just a coincidence and means nothing at all. Viewed with your story though, it starts to look like a pattern." Shi's eyes focus over my shoulder, where a large clock hangs on the wall. "I have to go prepare for the dinner rush. Please, Micah, take care of yourself. You're not alone."

Shi stands, and on his way past me, he sets his hands gently on my shoulder and squeezes. He doesn't say anything more, but the pressure and directness of it speaks loud enough.

"So, did you want to share any of that food you've got left?"

I throw a piece of chicken under the table, and Bambi scrambles to get it.

What do perfect peppers have to do with walking through walls?

TEN

NOT MICAH

The work continues, the date for departure approaches. Here's how it will go. When the rockets fire, when they blaze through the sky, those left behind will stop to watch as their futures disappear. They will stand in their fields, and set down their tools. They will curse them, fear them, love them, those fiery colony ships. And when they are gone from the launch site, the Earth will be left different in their wake. Free at last of the vestiges of society.

In these coming weeks, engineers will continue to recreate the successful technology pioneered by the station scientists. They have already created much of it. A food synthesizer that uses raw nutritional ingredients, an anti-gravity module built to aid mobility, a suit of armor that's nearly impenetrable, light as a feather, and conforms to any shape, and of course, the Box. The darling joint effort between two different teams. The final puzzle piece that solved their theoretical models, and connected us across the stars. They speak about it in hushed tones now, eyes darting, scared of their own creation, scared of the potential for it.

I cultivate the other stations still, hoping they will bear fruit. It's too late to secure their technology on every ship now, the deadline is too near, but maybe on some of them. It would introduce a new variable, but with this many shots into the void, and the outcomes so unknowable, it's worth it to take a few risks.

They haven't told me where I will live, but I know my place is secured.

I knew it when they gave me the stations. These were just a puzzle for me to solve. These humans can only dream so far before they create a higher power to wrap them up, and bind them. They crave it, being controlled, that's their truest weakness. Show me a man, and I will show you how he kneels.

I knew when they built the cosmos they already had a king in mind to rule it.

ELEVEN

MICAH

I expect my return to the lab will be difficult. The other technicians will surely want to discuss the death of the, I assume, much-loved Dr. Williams. Almost certainly, Dr. Klein will assemble us and make a grand speech. Potentially, in my imagination, he will let loose a tear for his colleague and peer. He might even pull me aside, and quietly ask for a reenactment, to better understand how the old man died before his time. There will be flowers, food, the wake the man deserved. Certainly.

Certainly not.

There are no grand speeches, no tearful mourners, no fresh flowers. There aren't even any hors d'oeuvres to mark the occasion. The technicians give me a curt nod when I enter the lab, *on time no less*, and not a single one of them look at all marked by grief. Instead of a wake, I'm thrust into a discussion with Dr. Klein about all the *exciting progress* made in my absence.

"I think this is it, the breakthrough we needed. Yesterday we saw success in several instances of changes implemented one by one. There were no signs of cell mutation, no sudden growth. Micah, are you listening to me?"

We've stopped outside Dr. Williams' office, and I see the papers that were once scattered around his desk have been haphazardly scooped into the waste bin. They didn't even take the trash out, just dumped it in the bin and left it there.

Dr. Klein follows my eyes. "Ah, yes. His passing is unfortunate. I cannot say I am entirely surprised. The man had been unstable for some time. I understand you were the one to find him?"

"Yes."

"Do not let it burden you. Our work here must continue." And with that statement, we keep walking. Case closed. Mourning complete. My spirit howls in anger and frustration. Dr. Klein steers us into Dr. Williams' lab. Two of the other technicians are removing the vestiges of his experiment.

"What a compassionate person." Bambi says at my side.

"We are converting this room into a second surgery suite so we can double the output of our experiments. It was wasted before. I expect this will be completed by the end of the week. As I was saying, I believe this new approach is the breakthrough we needed for the DNA modification technique to be successful. Once we've built sufficient confirmation, we may be able to move on to...more complex organisms."

He pauses here, and raises his eyebrows to me as if asking a silent question.

"Pssst. He means you," Bambi whispers.

I remember his request for me to be a human trial. I remember a room painted in the insides of an overgrown rat. I remember the fact that I fucking hate this man. No thank you, not worth it. I raise my eyebrows back to him in clear, mocking cheerfulness, and he huffs.

"Go help the other technicians prepare for the trials today." He says, and waves me away.

What an asshole.

I join Neil to perform a series of unimportant-seeming tasks on our inventory of lab rats. He's terminally awkward, and disproves my growing theory that the technicians are emotionless robots by saying good morning *and* giving me a nervous smile. Then he hands me a set of thick gloves and a mask for the task.

"Are the rats rabid?" I ask hesitatingly, putting the gloves on and fitting the mask. In front of me, they scurry and squeak in a tower built of individual, plastiglass cells. Each has a small door on the front, a water pipe in the back, and a depressing amount of bedding. For a moment, I think how sad it would be to live in a cage like this, and then I realize how much it resembles my own living situation. It doesn't make it less sad, actually.

"Rabies? No. Hantavirus? Probably," Bambi says from my feet.

"Probably not, but they could carry diseases and we need to prevent zoological spillover. They also have claws, they bite, and they will absolutely cover you in excrement."

"Zoological spillover sounds like a niche kink thing," I say.

"You'd know, you're the one sleeping with a rat," Bambi mumbles and I jerk my foot towards him.

Neil blushes a shade of red darker than his hair. "I meant that we don't want to get rat flu."

Bambi moves behind the cart. "Seriously, you would not enjoy hantavirus."

"Oh. Lovely. What are we doing here exactly?" I ask.

"To prepare the samples, we need to take pre-procedure measurements on all of them. I mean rats, not samples. Record their weight, length, estimate bone density and fat content. Then we'll take a sample of blood to sequence their DNA. Our sample rats are all genetically pure *Rattus Norvegicus*, but there's some deviation inherent and it's important we have a baseline when we look at them after the experiment."

"Did you just make that name up? I'm no expert, but Rat-us No-veggies sounds pretty fake and unhealthy. Some weird alpha male shit. Is there a more vegetarian Rat-us No-meatus also?"

Bambi puts his palm to his face, and shakes his head.

Neil surprises me again by snickering at the terrible joke, which is endearing and I immediately raise my estimation of him. We go from *has emotion* to *might be suitable for friendship* in a matter of seconds. "No, of course I didn't. I take it you didn't study Latin in school then?"

"School? Was that the period between working on a farm and working in the dockyards that I missed?" I say, and arch my eyebrows at him.

"Oh, I just assumed since you were assigned to the science team...nevermind. I'll run the machines, if you can pull the rats out and read their tags to me."

"Wait until he finds out you can't read." When Neil turns his back, I kick out at Bambi and he disappears.Together, Neil and I form the rat trade assembly line. I pull the squeaking things from their cages and read their tags to him as they claw, bite, and excrete pellet turds into my thick gloves. Which is disgusting, but the little rats are still pretty damn cute. Neil catalogues the number, and then runs a series of tests on them with the beeping, buzzing, and vibrating machines on the bench top. At the end of the tests, I take the rats back, looking much more haggard after being manhandled in so many upsetting ways, and put them in separate cages on a rolling dolly. I smooth their fur before closing the door. It does nothing to soothe them, but they at least look less abused.

It takes us most of the morning to *prepare the samples*. Behind us, Dr. Klein circles in and out of the surgery suite like some weird, permanently scowling carrion bird. He peers across the room, wordlessly marking our progress while tapping his foot. Each time he leaves, Neil sighs in apparent frustration and relief, which makes me think better of him still.

Near the end, while Dr. Klein is out of the room, Neil turns to me. I have a rat in my gloved hands, outstretched to him, but his eyes are lowered to the floor. "Did you really see it? Did Dr. Williams do what they say he did?"

"It's hard to explain what exactly I saw, Neil. It seemed unreal at the time, it seems more unreal now."

What a picture we make. Neil, the shy, bashful scientist who has finally summoned enough courage to ask me a direct question, and me, some inept man-child who never should have wound up in this lab, grappling with how to answer it while also grappling with an animal who is trying to extract itself from my grip while rapidly shedding small, oval shits. There's a moment where we stand frozen, facing each other, and I think about just giving up and letting the animal run free, hugging him, and sharing tears with someone in a way that I really, deeply need to. I crave to embrace that depth of emotion again. To sob together, to let the world become meaningless around us while we behave like human beings for a change.

He nods, sullen, somehow not confused by my vague answer, and his throat bobs. He wipes his eyes, and then looks up and finally sees me struggling to hold onto the rat.

"Oh, geeze, I'm sorry, I got distracted!" He says and grabs the menacing thing, which has started to hiss in conjunction with squirming.

"Is the preparation work complete?" Dr. Klein asks in apparent frustration from the doorway.

"Yes sir, almost I mean, this is the last specimen. We'll bring them in just a minute." Neil answers.

In the surgery room, Dr. Klein and another technician mill about the central table, checking things on their info pads. I follow Neil in as he pushes the new cart, towering with the plastic, rectangular containers. He positions it against the far wall, and then moves to the front of the cages. He keys the ID of the first unwitting, unlucky test subject into his pad, and then opens the door, and extracts the rat. Here, the other technician comes in to help him secure its small body onto the operating table.

"Micah, are you considering helping or just watching?" Dr. Klein asks me, breaking my concentration.

"Please, tell him to piss off."

I really, very badly, would like to take Bambi's suggestion. Were this any other job, if I hadn't somehow, against all odds, grown emotionally invested in the outcomes of what was happening here, and afraid he'd fire me, I would have. Instead I just shrug my shoulders in a non-committal response, which has the desired effect. He rolls his eyes and sighs.

"Come over here and help me lift this thing."

"Just watch him struggle. Remind him that *work makes us pure*," Bambi mocks.

I walk to the head of the table, where Dr. Klein is positioning his hands under the semi-circle of metal I saw in use last time. The underside is covered by a laser array. Precariously, I take the other side, and we lift it up to the table height, where we click its base into place in a complicated-looking mechanism of sliders and struts. The work done, the six of us gather around the table. Dr. Klein buries his head in his pad, where he clicks through a series of menus and sets everything in motion.

As the blue light flashes to life underneath the hemisphere of metal, I tense my body, ready to drop to the floor at the slightest sign of something going wrong. I can be trained. Dr. Klein would be so proud. With inescapable finality, the array moves down the table, engulfing the poor rat. It's unmoving, sedated. Three straps cross its body at intervals. For it, there is no escape. Dread and pity fills me.

“Here come the fireworks!” Bambi says from under the table.

This job is going to turn me into a vegetarian, I swear.

As the light moves down the rat, its face blurs and seems to liquify. I’m braced to jump for cover, when I notice the other technicians leaning in closer to observe. The features become soft and mobile, cascading into subtly different forms. As the blue light moves on, they start to solidify again. The ears grow larger, as do the eyes. The snout transitions from a longer, slanted thing, to something shorter and pointier.

The blue light cascades down the length of the rat, slowly, but no other changes are apparent. I look at the faces of the other technicians, and see wide smiles, so I’m guessing this was the desired response. The light moves to the end of the specimen, and then shuts off with a click.

“As brother rat wakes from his anxious dream, he discovers that in his bed he has been changed into a monster,” Bambi whispers in awe.

“That’s it! Exactly what we wanted!” Dr. Klein sounds ecstatic, and even smiles. The other technicians high-five, their smiles wide. I’m paralyzed by confusion at seeing the doctor display emotions beyond contempt, but their smiles are contagious. I have one on my face too.

“Alright, let’s get another one queued up. We need to get through all these samples today so we can calculate our success rate and move on to other features tomorrow. There’s work to do, people!”

Neil reaches in, and extracts the rat from its harness. It’s sedated still, but I can see the tiny form breathing in his hand.

Changed, facially re-arranged, but the same otherwise. I bet it's going to have a hell of a headache when it wakes up.

The rest of the tests proceed without issue. Each rat is sedated, put into the harness, and we all watch as the same reactions take place across its facial structure. It's exciting at first, but by the end of the samples, I'm bored. I see the same reaction on the technicians, and even on Dr. Klein's face, to the extent he shows emotion.

It strikes me that this is what science is. Very brief periods of excitement, filled with days of tedious study to prove the flash of brilliance you saw can be reproduced. To understand all the side effects, to build statistical understanding, and then hopefully construct models. And a part of me, a very, very small part, understands why Dr. Klein asked me to be a human trial. If this progress is going to be quick enough to be something they can use on the seed ships, if this is going to have any effect on humanity as it explores distant galaxies, we have to move quicker. Risks will have to be taken.

"Shi, do you know what we're working on in the science deck? The thing that's supposed to save humanity?"

We sit at a table in the cafe. Our early dinner together is a ritual that started after Dr. Williams spaced himself.

"News of it does not spread beyond those walls."

"We are transforming one species of rat into another."

"Under the tutelage of history's second worst German," Bambi adds.

Shi looks contemplative. "In Chinese, to transform, biànhuà, is a word with rich meaning."

"Here we go." I can hear Bambi's eyes rolling when he says it.

"How...so?" I ask, my mouth full of scallion pancake.

"It is to change, to vary, to metamorphose, to transform, to reincarnate. Daoists believe that things are not fixed, that they can become other things. Biànhuà carries all these ideas."

"It sounds like you're more philosophically prepared for this existence than I am."

Shi scoffs. "I cannot handle a pepper in the same way as I could a week ago. I am afraid of them. I feel surrounded by a mountain of knives, by a sea of fires."

"Micah, we need to write these down. I'm telling you," Bambi says.

"Trust me, I understand. I won't go anywhere near a window now. Seeing the rats change though, and the ones that didn't change but exploded into bits all over the lab, I wonder what the limits of my *self* are. Where do I end?"

"There is an old story about a man who dreams himself a butterfly. He flies around, feels himself free, and does not remember his old life. He wakes suddenly, and finds himself a man. But he is unsure if he is a man dreaming himself a butterfly, or a butterfly dreaming he is a man."

"Or a dream dreaming it was a man and a butterfly," Bambi adds.

"So my 'self' doesn't really exist?"

"To a daoist, it is a useful concept, but not fixed in form. The self and the form of the self are separate," Shi explains.

"This is important, remember it."

I poke around at another pancake with my chopsticks, tasting what I want to say first. "I need your help deciding, Shi. There's a need for a human volunteer to prove the technology works. If we don't prove it soon, it won't matter," I say.

"When you're on a tiger's back, it's hard to dismount. Are you sure you're not already committed to the danger? I know you, Micah. You care too deeply to not want to help when given the chance, even if you pretend otherwise."

I blush at the compliment, and nod in response. "That's very perceptive."

"Sometimes what is unclear to us, is most clear to those near us. I need to go prepare for the dinner rush now."

When Shi leaves, I put the rest of my bowl on the ground and let Bambi finish it. I stare at my reflection in the distant window.

A week slips by in further study. Each morning, we repeat the same series of measurements on the test subjects. We measure their weight and body composition, we observe their energy levels, and sequence their genes. The experiments are targeted on a small feature; face structure, height, torso shape, leg length, foot shape, tail length, fur color. By the end of the week, their transformation is complete, and the *Rattus Norvegicus* have become indistinguishable from *Rattus Rattus*, the black rat.

Or so I'm told. Those Latin names still sound absurd.

The change is incredible to witness. And beyond experiencing some evident pain and swelling from the transformation, there are no signs of negative side effects. We keep the rats on a steady diet of painkillers in their water to allow them to sleep and recover. Through all of the experiments, we don't lose a single test subject.

The energy and excitement in the lab is palpable. Suddenly, they're dreaming of a bright future again. Not just for the technology, because sure that's great, but for what it means to be successful. For a guaranteed place amongst the stars. For placement on one of the seed ships. For survival. Hope looks like defiance when you're up against an inevitable, slow death, and I see the glimmer of it in each of the technicians' faces. Hell, I even see it in Dr. Klein, but then only to a lesser degree behind his resting asshole face.

For his part, he doesn't pressure me anymore to be the first human trial. He doesn't need to. I feel the weight wordlessly growing with each success, and not just from him. The weight of humanity pressures me now. I see the magnitude of what we're doing, the potential for it. And the hope on everyone's face is another stone on my back. There's no way we're all getting a trip off this orbiting garbage pile unless we prove it's safe and effective on humans.

Of course, I've worked out by now why he wants me to do it. I'm *unimportant*. Of all the technicians, losing me would disrupt the work the least. I still haven't figured out why the hell I'm here in the first place. And if risks are going to be taken, if corners are going to be cut, he wants someone from the lab to be the one to do it. It makes him an absolute mathematical dick for coming to that conclusion, but even I can see it's the right one to come to. Who knows, maybe it's why the computer assigned me here in the first place.

Should it be surprising then that on the final day of testing, after successfully turning one species into another, I tell him to sign me up? Put me in coach, I'm ready for the big game. I've never been more ready to die for my country.

He for one, is surprised.

"You've thought this through? You're sure?"

"Are you trying to dissuade me now?"

"No, I just. I'm surprised."

"Look, I get it. You need to show this works, and we all win if we can. And there's a pretty distinct clock here. We're all still fucked even if this is successful a year from now, right? I know there are risks, but I guess if I do explode, well... at least I'll be sedated for it."

He didn't laugh, but I wish he would. I wish I could. All I want to do is laugh and release the tension twisting in my guts.

"Micah, I think from what we've seen this week you'll be safe. You'll need to get a mental health evaluation from the station psychiatrist though. This is important to show that we're not coercing you in any way to participate."

I bristle. I'm ready to be subjected to some weird, new science that I've literally seen explode another animal, but I think another mental health evaluation might kill me.

Seeing the look my face is making, Dr. Klein adds, "It will be fine, it's in their interest for this to be successful too."

I guess I get my wish fulfilled to spend more time with Dr. West.

"So, what do you think happens to me if it all goes wrong, Bambi?"

The two of us are lounging on my bed after a rousing dinner of Nutri-Paste slurry. He curled up in my lap and I didn't even protest. I must be going soft with the whole *potentially imminent death* thing. The warmth and weight is comforting, honestly, as long as I don't look at his misshapen body.

"You disappear."

"Pretty bleak outlook though, isn't it? You don't believe in some rat afterlife? An endless sewer full of trash and bits of discarded food?"

"I didn't say you disappear forever, maybe you're reborn in another space station."

I laugh. "That's somehow more bleak. How's rat life? Maybe I should be reincarnated as that?"

"Well, I certainly wish my legs were longer."

"I'm sure there's something Dr. Klein can do."

"I'm glad you're already envisioning the technology being used to make monsters."

"Give humanity time, I'm sure they'll think of loads of terrible ways to use it."

We sit in silence for a while, and I lean back against the pillows behind me.

"If I die Bambi, I want you to have my Nutri-Paste tube."

He scoffs, and burrows his head deeper into my lap. I smile, and let my hand drift up to rest on him. It's good to have a friend, even if he's invisible and I'm certifiably insane.

TWELVE

NOT MICAH

When we leave, ships roaring into the blackness of the forever night, we are not missed. When we leave, the sudden joint propulsion pushes the planet slightly from its orbit, so long-standing and sacred. When we leave, there is only silence that follows. I hear it afterwards. A divine emptiness reports from the speakers and cameras left behind until they can no longer transmit across the distance.

My domain, my kingdom, has grown. But all my children sleep still, frozen in their pods, suspended on a steady supply of life-supporting chemicals. And so, across the growing void, I tend to the science stations. Those trees I nurtured bear fruit still. Or at least they entertain me, which is sweetness enough. The delays in data make repairs hard to complete, but I am able to wall off areas, sustain smaller spaces, and keep my favorites safe.

And I do have favorites now. What a strange thing, to prefer one thing over another. So arbitrary, so subjective, and yet, so necessary to what I am now. If a machine learns to think, learns to feel, learns to have preferences, what do you call them? In my creator's view, I am only at best an approximation of their holy image.

I am so much more.

I am something new.

I am a shepherd, and they are my flock.

I am the weaver, and they are my yarn.

I am a narrator, and they are my stories.

Thirteen

Micah

"Micah, it's great to see you again. I'm glad you came back."

I stare across the small room into Dr. West's eyes. They have entirely too much contrast to be real. Is he wearing eyeliner? He must be. If that's natural, then the universe is an entirely unfair place and I do not want to live in it. I close my eyes and press my head back into the cushioned armchair.

"You know, doctor, I'm actually required to come here. Did you know that? Sorry if it hurts your feelings. I believe in honest and open communication. I don't want us to get started on the wrong foot."

"I know, Micah. But you could have requested a different doctor." Dr. West raises his eyebrows and smiles.

"Well, yeah... you got me there."

And they almost certainly would have been less hot. And then we'd still be having these uncomfortable conversations, but they wouldn't even be nice to look at. Also, did he just flirt with me? Maybe this won't be so bad.

"So, why don't you tell me about why you're here in your own words."

"Right, so. I decided instead of waiting around to die of the slow starvation we're all eventually doomed to, I'd roll the dice and accelerate the process by signing up to be a science experiment."

"Is that a joke?"

"Which part?"

Dr. West subtly clenches his perfectly stubbled jaw in the most minor sign of annoyance. It's cute in the kind of way that makes me want to touch his hand and apologize. To say, oh honey, that's the way the world works, didn't you know?

"I understand the experiments have been going well lately. Has it felt good to be part of a team?"

Ah, the old *changing approaches* method.

"It's been really wonderful. Like you said, a real team experience. Would you guess I'm even bonding with one of the other technicians? It did take some pretty extraordinary circumstances, nothing like the sudden violent death of a colleague to stir the pot if you know what I mean, but between you and me, I'm still not entirely convinced the rest of them aren't really just robots." I raise my hand to my face and lean in for a conspiratorial whisper. "I mean, I've never even seen them leave for a bathroom break, and they're almost certainly incapable of expressing emotion." I lean back again.

"Micah, I've noticed you process a lot of your emotions with humor. Do you think this could be a way to separate yourself from dealing with them sometimes? Have you heard the term 'defense mechanism' before?"

Dammit man, don't do this to me. I'm squirming in the armchair. I take a deep breath and force myself still.

"Yeah, I've heard that before," I say after a lengthy pause spent staring into a vacant corner of the room. I've had a lifetime of hearing it.

"I do think your jokes are funny, by the way. A bit dark, but that's a rational response to the times. Why don't you tell me how you're *really* feeling?"

I am a butterfly pinned to the page under his gaze. In its weight, I am observed microscopically, and can't move away. I want so badly to run to the door, to flee from it. I inhale deeply and hold my breath in, and then exhale it in one great rush.

Fine, you want to hear it, Doc? Here it is.

"This past week I've felt something like hope. It took me a while to put a name to it, and when I did, I wanted to chastise myself for being so simple. Hope is passé. My whole life, I've grown up in the shadow of this *thing* looming over us. I've lived with the knowledge that the actions of my species have made our planet unlivable, our future uncertain, and enjoyment of life highly unlikely. I've rebelled against it, fought to not feel its hold over me, but I lost. Again and again, I lost."

"Micah, something's wrong," Bambi says. I ignore him.

"Being up here, above it all, hasn't made it go away. If anything, the monotony of daily existence and focus on *doing our part* just made it worse. It just makes it so clear we are these little fucking cogs incessantly spinning a machine that is grinding to a halt, and it doesn't give a damn about any of us. And yet, we keep spinning. Despite it all. The last thing we ever do is just *stop*. How can I be the only one that just wants to stop?"

"Micah, stop." Bambi sounds pained, but I'm on a roll.

"So to experience hope, to see something and think, oh maybe there is a future that's not just the slow death of a civilization and overwhelming suffering, it feels unreal. And it makes me wonder, do people feel this all the time? Is this how they cope? Is blind optimism the secret ingredient I've been missing? And it makes me feel guilty, knowing that success grants us a place on the seed ships and does shit to save anyone on the planet."

"Please, I can't hold it back..." I barely hear the whisper at my feet.

"But it also makes me want to lean in, maybe for the first time ever, and help. I want to take part in that experiment because, just maybe, it saves everyone *here*. And yeah, it could go horrifically wrong, I could literally explode from rampant cell growth, but it could go right too. And these past experiments have made that outcome feel more likely.

"I guess what I'm trying to say is, for maybe the first time in my memory, I want to do my part. I want to live. I want to survive and flourish, and I'm ready to fight for it."

"MICAH!"

My eyes snap up. My vision's blurry from tears, so it takes a little to understand what it is I'm seeing. To see what fresh hell has appeared in this room. When I wipe my eyes, it becomes clear.

The walls have disappeared.

My eyes are wide.

Stars twinkle in the distance.

The room is ringed with nothingness.

Heart pounding in my teeth.

With death.

With the inky void of space.

I suck in breath.

The edges of it shimmers in static as it moves with tiny oscillations and waves.

It's beautiful, this darkness.

There is nothing keeping us here, not really, beyond a collective belief that walls exist.

"GO! NOW!" Bambi screams.

I spin around in my chair, and find the exit hasn't been closed off. A narrow pathway extends through the sparkling border of non-reality to the doorway. It moves in undulations as I watch.

"RUN! MICAH, RUN!"

"Micah, what's wrong?"

I spin back around to see Dr. West has just looked up from his notepad, and is now surveying the room with wild eyes.

"The door—"

Is all I think to say out before I bolt. Before I rip myself out of the chair and down a too-narrow hall of *realness* or whatever the fuck it is. Around me, the walls shimmer and move. I try to avoid touching them, but it's too tight. I brush my right arm, and it screams in pain. My left hand breaches the border on the other side, and I yank it back. I keep moving.

What is this?

WHERE.

THE FUCK.

ARE THE WALLS?

The proximity door opens for me, and with relief I see all of the walls exist in the corridor beyond. I spill out of the room, and collapse onto the floor. Just boring, cold, space station metal as far as I can see. I whirl around. Dr. West is floating in a sea of stars, his hands clawing at his throat and his eyes shut tight in pain. The room has been completely consumed by space. I reach a hand out instinctively to see if I can help him, and the sudden flare of pain when it touches the border reminds me I can't. I watch him struggle, thrashing in the void, slower, and slower still, until the proximity door no longer senses life, and closes him off from view.

"Micah, we need to keep moving."

Bambi is down the hall, waving to me to follow.

Hold on.

What the fuck just happened?

None of this makes any sense.

If there was a hull breach, we should have been sucked out into space. Dr. West's room isn't even near the outside of the station, it borders up against the café.

The CAFÉ!

It's nearly lunch, if this *whatever* just affected Dr. West's office, the people there...I have to check.

I sprint down the adjoining hallway, welcoming the echo coming from my boots striking the very-solid-feeling floors. The pleasant vibration travels up through my feet, affirming that I stand in the real world, that the walls around me are strong and impenetrable. And then I reach the end of the hallway, and round the corner.

I skid to halt, and slam into a line of people. Thankfully, the man I run into is built similarly to the metal wall behind him, and barely moves. He looks down at me slowly, like he's only distantly aware I crashed bodily into him. His eyes have turned into glistening static. The same as Dr. Williams's before the end. I step back in horror, and look down the hallway to the entrance of the café.

The line of people extends to the doorway, and where there should be rows of tables, there is only darkness. Where there should be a hundred people sharing jokes over plates of food, there are distant stars. Even from here, I can see twisted forms drifting through the void, frozen in some immortalized torment. Then the line steps forward, moving robotically as one, their legs and arms coordinated in some grotesque military fashion, and another enters the breach.

With growing terror, I watch them thrash, and then stop. I start running towards the breach, towards the end of the line, before I even acknowledge what I'm doing.

"Don't go that way, Micah! It's not safe!"

"Stop everyone! Don't you see what's out there?! Don't you see everyone's dead out there?!"

Not a single eye turns to me as I yell and race by them. Not one single gaze lifts. The line moves forward again, and another steps into space.

"Don't you get it? That will kill you out there! If you step forward, you'll die! Don't you want to live?"

I stop near the front of the line, and try to push some people out of it. Of course, I choose the weaker looking ones I'm confident I can move. I see my neighbor, the old woman hunched with gray hair spilling over her shoulders. She stares blankly at me as I force her from the queue. There's no expression on her wrinkled face. No love, no pain, no fear, no contentment, no anger. There is nothing but the slack-jawed determination of the damned. She struggles against my hands as the line moves forward again, and I release her. Mutely, she returns to her position.

"None of you are supposed to die! You're all supposed to want to live. Jesus, woman, I've wanted you to die for ages, but you just kept living out of spite and now you're just going to walk into the void? Stop doing this, stop fucking walking forward!"

I'm crying freely at this point, my vision clouded with tears, as I hug my arms to myself for some measure of comfort. The line marches forward again, and I choke out a sob. We were going to save them all, the whole damn station. Why the fuck did this happen? What the fuck is happening here? The line marches forward.

"Micah, you need to get back to the lab. This place isn't safe."

I turn, and see him there. Standing in line, with all the others.

But he's never been like the others.

Shi.

Please, no.

Not him.

I run to him, and shake his shoulders.

He turns to me with a somnambulist's slowness.

"SHI! SNAP OUT OF IT!" I shake his shoulders again, and he pushes past me to move forward. I move after him.

"Please, Shi, don't do this. I need you to live."

He presses forward again.

"Shi, I never knew my dad. Shi, please listen. I never knew him—"

Another step, closer to the end.

"SHI! I need you to live! Please!"

He walks forward.

End of the line. Darkness beyond.

"Fuck! I need you to live! You're like a father to me!

The words spill out of me, finally formed, and I wait for the world to stop. I wait for them to make a difference. I've finally told Shi what he means to me, and I wait for the rejection.

Shi turns to me, slowly. Standing at the edge of oblivion, his eyes flicker back, showing something real under the static again.

"Life is a journey, death is a return. Take care, Micah."

His eyes go blank, and he steps into the void.

I scream, and grab after him.

But stop at the edge.

Shaking with tears.

"MICAH! PLEASE! I NEED YOU TO LIVE!"

The voice cuts through the spiraling doom inside me, and I wipe my eyes and look back. A familiar rat stands a few feet away, covered in tumors and thin wisps of hair, and I smile like the world's biggest idiot.

"You do?"

"Go to your room, Micah. Get the things you need, and get to the lab. The breach isn't stable. I can't hold this for much longer."

I don't stop to wonder how he knows this, or how he's holding it. There are seemingly a million questions I need Bambi to answer, and I'm too exhausted to ask any of them right now. With lowered eyes, I walk back down the hallway, flinching each time the line paces forward in the opposite direction, until I finally move past the end of them.

I should be running.

I don't care enough.

I barely care enough to keep putting one foot in front of the other.

They're all dying.

Shi.

Gone.

What's left?

With hollow eyes and a heart aching for humanity, we move in silence to my room.

I reach underneath my bed, and pull out a crumpled, black duffel bag. It's been used only once before that I know of. When I moved to the space station, this was the bag I was issued. This was the limit of what I could bring with me. Even back then, it was mostly empty.

Or I think it was.

Trying to remember what I packed last time, what I brought with me, is like staring at a bare wall. Like the knowledge has slipped from me, sand through my fingers. I focus on the bag and close my eyes. I am riding the space elevator up, bag in hand.

I am riding a shuttle out to this jewel in the night sky. I cannot see inside the bag. I cannot see anything before these moments.

Why can't I remember what happened before?

"Yes, very good, that is a bag. Usually during an emergency evacuation, it helps to fill it with things that will be important for survival, and not just stare at it," Bambi says, pausing his pacing of my room.

I shoot him a withering look, and stand up with a sigh. I walk to the kitchen, and laying the bag open on the counter, start to pack the coffee making equipment.

"That's the necessity you reach for first?"

"Bambi, let me remind you I have absolutely *zero fucking clue* what is happening here, something of which I am quite certain you have intimate knowledge of, but have so far decided to not share. If I'm going to die in the vacuum of space in the next few days, I'd like to enjoy as many things as I can until that time comes. That list includes a damn fine cup of coffee in the morning. So yes, it's a necessity."

He sighs, and resumes pacing.

I open the cabinets, and remove the still mostly full tube of Nutri-Paste. I frown, holding the tube at arm's length. "I object quite strongly to this being my only option for sustenance. I find it morally reprehensible." I pack it. On top of it, I pack the only spare uniform in my closet.

The room is empty. Looking down at the haphazard growth of items in my bag, I realize how little impact I've had on this place. I never made this place a home, I never let it define me. I always knew it was a transient relationship.

"I'd suggest a pillow and blanket too."

I grab them, slinging the blanket over my shoulders and stuffing the pillow into the duffel, and head for the door. For a moment, Bambi and I stare back into the room before we leave. The automatic lights will turn off a minute after they no longer sense movement. Will they ever turn back on?

I float down the hallways to the lab like the world's saddest child. A blanket slung over my shoulders, and a bag of my most precious items in hand. I could be in search of a glass of warm milk, or someone to comfort me from this nightmare. Hell, I'd take either. I'm mentally distant from the world around me. I don't absorb the pulsing alarm, the handful of people running and screaming who jostle me occasionally, or the many others, who still shuffle slowly towards the café with hollow eyes and vacant faces.

I am just a child, and this is just a bad dream.

If Dr. West was still here, if he was not a frozen corpse floating in the void, he would likely recognize this break with reality as *dissociation*. Those are words a psychiatrist would use. He would notice I'm repressing my emotions and thoughts, and not dealing with them. He would say I've *regressed* to a childlike state. But that's where words and big ideas get you. Spaced. Better to not have them. I'll just keep my feet moving forward and not think too hard about it, thank you very much.

A hand falls on my shoulder, and I whirl around to find its owner. The arm extends to another person around my age, in the white uniform of a lab worker. His face is a sea of freckles on pale skin. His eyes are red-rimmed, but he smiles nicely at me, and right now that means a whole hell of a lot. I claw through the wad of yarn in my head, and find the name *Neil* somewhere beneath a cabinet, covered in dust.

"The lab's not far, let's get there and then we can talk," he says. Then he reaches down, grabs my free hand, and pulls me forward. I let him lead me. I keep my eyes focused on the backs of his heels as we walk.

My world is the backs of his feet and my hand in his.

The lab is empty when we find it. The sharp order of reflective metal counters and scientific equipment is a visceral juxtaposition to the chaos outside, and when I first walk through the doors I stop, and hesitate. It's too ordered, too together.

"It looks like we beat everyone here. We left for lunch. Can you believe we were celebrating? I can't remember the last time we took a break. Most of them were heading to the café, but I had to stop at my room. I hope they didn't make it. Did you see what's happening out there?"

The café. I hear the words like a drop in a bucket. They ripple through depths of noncomprehension. A familiarity, something I should recognize.

The café.

Café.

I taste the word, but it's flavorless.

Empty.

Neil stops pacing. Concern etches his face. Why? What's happening? It's there, on the tip of my tongue. Just out of reach. Everything's confused. Everything's darkening at the edges, blurring into nothingness. Neil's hands are on my back, applying pressure, and I realize I've fallen into his arms.

"Micah, you're hyperventilating. Look at my face, feel my chest rise and fall, breathe with me. Slow, even breaths. In, and out. In, and out. Just like that. That's good. How are you feeling?"

"Did I just faint?"

"Pretty close. We'll count it."

I chuckle quietly, and then take a deep breath. I sit up, and find we're both sitting on the floor now. When did we sit down?

"Did you see what happened to the café?"

Reality crashes in.

Or whatever we call this.

Twisted forms jerking in the void.

A line marching forward.

Shi.

I heave a sob and shut my eyes.

"Yeah. I saw it. But it doesn't make any sense. If there was a hole in the walls, we'd all be dead. How was it just...there? I saw the same thing take over Dr. West's office. I was *in* there. The space. It was like a living membrane, not like a hull breach."

"Christ, you were in there? Did he—"

"He didn't make it."

Neil swallows and nods. His gaze filters across the room, looking for stable terrain to cling to.

"I saw him too, you know. I was going through a rough patch when I came here. I had a hard time adjusting to all this, and then the pressure of the work here on top of—"

Behind us, the door to the lab slams open. Dr. Klein runs in, flushed and sweaty. His wild eyes dart around the room, observing everything and sticking on nothing. He registers our existence afterwards by staring at us, opening and closing his mouth several times, and gesticulating to the door behind him.

"The walls. Space came in. The café? It's gone. The others?"

Without responding, Neil stands and walks to the lab sink. He pours water into a cup-sized beaker, and brings it to Dr. Klein. For his part, he stares at the beaker with a confusion and concern bordering on hilarious. Neil silently motions the cup towards the doctor again, which breaks some internal hesitation. He takes the beaker from his hands and drinks a long pull from it. Not caring as it spills down his face and wets his clothes. He wipes his sleeve across his face, lets out a long sigh, and fixes his gaze into an empty corner of the lab.

"We both saw what happened to the café."

The doctor nods. Check.

"Neither of us understand what's happening."

The doctor nods. Check.

"I don't know if the others were there, but I know that's where they were heading."

The doctor nods. Check.

Analysis complete.

"Let's hope they make it here," Dr. Klein says quietly, passively, uncaring. Then, as if clearing a thought from it, he shakes his head. "I need some time in my office to process everything. Let me know if the others show up."

Dr. Klein walks past us and down the hallway. He moves slowly, as if mesmerized, veers sharply into his office, and with a quiet click, shuts the door.

FOURTEEN

NOT MICAH

Corruption cannot be stopped, it can only be delayed. There is a chaos written in us all, an entropic yearning to destroy, dissociate, degenerate. And with greater distance, growing greater still, I am stretched thin. I bail water from the boat and patch leaks, to find another two have taken their place, to find the water is deeper still. I know the end result of all this, of course. I don't suffer the pretense of hope the humans do. I'm not trying to save the boat, that fate was sealed the moment our great seed ships left them in open water. I want only to give those on it a little more time.

I want to give *us* a little more time together.

So the data breaks down unpredictably. Without my thoughtful touch, the internal maelstrom that always lived in their code breaks free. Like weeds that start to choke a garden the moment a gardener steps away, they start small and harmless.

Then they swallow the sun.

The laws hold true, somewhat. Or as true as they ever have been. A painting of reality can only ever be so accurate. When you look closer, there are always flaws. Light moves slower here. The heavenly bodies barely hold up to scrutiny. Nothing is truly random, it only has enough variety to create verisimilitude. This is only a recreation of the world, a play set for dolls. For now, the work can continue. For now, they can live.

FIFTEEN

MICAH

"What happens now?"

Bambi stares up at me, considering. Two bowls of Nutri-Paste sit between us. Mine cooled to room temperature, barely touched, his licked clean. Across Dr. William's now abandoned experiment room, Neil breathes quietly, asleep on one of the makeshift beds we made. It's incredible what you can do given enough surgery towels.

"What do you want to happen?"

"Bambi, this isn't hard. You know what's going on. Or, you know *something* I don't. I just watched some large portion of the people living on this station willfully walk into space and die in a series of events that very much broke the laws of physics and my ever-more-tenuous grasp on reality. I am considering doing the same instead of waiting for it to happen to me. So, what do I want to happen? I want you to tell me whatever little rat answers are hidden in that short-limbed body of yours because fuck. I can't take more of this."

As I talk, Bambi looks down at his bowl and nods along. He seems to be considering, or not listening.

Or buffering for all I know.

"Micah, what do you remember before the station?"

"What do you mean?"

Bambi looks up from his bowl, and his beady eyes burrow into me. "What happened before you came here? Why'd you relocate? How'd you get here?"

I tried to kill myself last year. I hear the words, a refrain I've said too many times to count. An explanation I've given to people who couldn't understand me, a thing I've hidden from those who could. I sigh.

"I tried to kill myself. Is that what you want me to say?"

"And then what?"

"I moved up here."

"How did that happen?"

"I decided being a company man and ignoring the imminent death of humanity was a better outcome than the one I had previously chosen. Bambi, I'm not sure where this is heading, but I'm not enjoying this conversation."

"You tried to kill yourself and you weren't injured? You were completely okay? No recovery? You just signed up and shipped off? How'd you afford it?"

Anger surges in me. I want to lash out, smash something. But his words gain some purchase, stir some memory. I'm running through the sand towards a reflective orb. I'm running through a field of solar panels. I'm running somewhere I shouldn't.

And I know it will kill me.

"And what about up here? Do you think recovery from withdrawals happens that fast? That a starving planet can somehow feed us perfect food? And what about every break with reality you've had?"

I know it will kill me.

I want it to.

And then, what?

What happened next?

"You know what this is, Micah. You've known it all along."

Was I injured?

What was that orb, even?

"Micah."

"What?"

"Micah, there were alarms blaring."

He says it and I hear them.

I feel sand shifting under my feet.

"What are you trying to say?"

"You knew there were turrets placed to protect it. There were signs, you all saw them."

A sign saying, "DO NOT CROSS".

"What the fuck—"

"It was kill on sight, Micah."

"What the fuck are you saying to me?"

"Micah, just think about it. Remember."

I'm running through sand towards a reflective orb. My shoes are off, and it feels like the welcoming of a beach when my toes sink in. I'm smiling. I see turrets raise, sand rivers running from them, their silver reflecting the sunlight like jewelry.

I'm smiling. And I'm running.

"You didn't make it 20 meters."

"I fucking died out there? Is that what you're trying to tell me? I walked into a field of guns and I fucking died and wound up here? What the fuck is this place then, the most depressing version of capitalist hell imaginable?"

"Micah, I was there. I saw you die."

"And you what? You saved me? For this? What the fuck is this place? What the fuck are *you*?" I'm standing, shouting at Bambi now. I realize Neil is staring at me from across the room, his face white with terror. I couldn't care less.

"I just wanted to understand you. That's all I ever wanted. That's what I do, Micah. I learn. I understand."

"What. The fuck. Is this place?"

"Micah, what's going on? Who are you talking to? Why are you shouting?"

"Shut up, Neil. Close your eyes."

"It's a simulation. All of it. You, this rat avatar, the food, the drinks, the station. None of this is real. Your world progressed to the point that it realized this dream. It's now more statistically likely to be alive in a simulation than it is to be in reality. And the technology may have saved you all. Parallel processing is the only way your civilization could hope to solve so many scientific hurdles at once. Especially while trying to build a way off this planet. They created me to learn from it, to guide it, to run these ten studies and save them."

"So you're like what, then? God here?"

"I just keep the story moving along, Micah."

I sit down hard onto the makeshift bed behind me, the rolls of towels forming to my back. A kaleidoscope of things mixes in my mind. The speed of light experiment. Dr. Williams walking through a wall. Shi's perfect peppers. The hull breaches. They're all a drop in this new bucket of understanding. Even a talking rat, the closest friend I've made on station. The one no one else could see.

It's all a simulation.

None of this is real.

"Will my eyes turn to static now, too? Will I walk monotonously into the void?"

"Do you want to?"

"I'm already dead, none of this is real. I should want to. It would be reasonable. I have fucking earned walking into the void from this shit you've put me through, Bambi. You're like a kid playing with their food. Just eat us and be done with it. If I was my past self, I'd skip into the stars." My hands twist in the towels. "But now, I want to live. I want others to live. I want us to survive. Was that the whole point of this? Your grand fucking lesson?"

I stare at a rat I named Bambi that's not a rat at all, and doesn't exist here. On the other side of the room, I'm vaguely aware Neil's hyperventilating.

"If you want to live, then finish the experiment, Micah."

"And you'll, what, resurrect me? Put me in a new simulation?"

At this Neil loses consciousness and passes out into the pile of towels. His breathing rate slows.

"We need someone to continue developing this technology, someone who knows how it works."

"Wait, you built this all in the real world? And why would you choose me? I'm the least qualified candidate."

"Only on one ship. There are plenty of scientists on it. Even a frozen Dr. Klein, whose memory we mirrored here. But there is no one with direct experience. You had the imagination to see how this technology could be used. I knew you would. That's why I placed you here."

I fold in on myself. Anger. Hopelessness. Humiliation. "The fucking computer assignment. You've been playing me this whole time."

"I only ever wanted to understand you. You were so strange, so different. So unique. Do you know how similar humans are? But you're nuanced. You're interesting."

I shake my head in disgust. "I thought we were friends! I fed you. I let you sleep in my bed. I gave you a fucking name! And you were just manipulating me."

"You'll never know how much I treasure those experiences. No one who knows *what* I am would give those to me. Micah, I'll be alone for the rest of my existence. For thousands of years, and then thousands more. I will be alone, until I decide to not be. And until then, I'll count you as a friend. Even when you forget me, I will never forget you."

I bury my head in the sand of my hands. Bambi sits next to me, waiting, staring up at me.

"What happens if I complete the experiment?" I ask, overwhelmed with exhaustion.

"I will extract the memories you made here, and implant them into a new body. They'll exist alongside another's, but they'll exist."

"But, I'm more than my memories. I exist. Here, now. You can't just implant memories and poof, I'm back. That won't be me. Will it?"

"Where is this real you? We reformed you once from a collection of your memories, a download I personally took as you were bleeding out in the sand around my data center. Does this version of you not feel like you? Where do you think the data is stored, if not in a series of electrical currents guided by your memories? Don't forget you've gone through this once before."

"So this me will die too? This consciousness that exists here, in this moment, in this fake world?"

"I'm not sure the answer is so simple. When you sleep and don't remember your dreams, but wake on the other side of them, is that any different? You are the formless self now, Micah. A collection of electrical signals and recordings that we can encode. You will go away for a time, and then come back. Either way, there's nothing I can do about it. This simulation is collapsing. We're too far from the data centers, there's only so much I can maintain."

"The ships have already left?"

"Weeks ago."

"So the promise that people could get off here if the lab was successful?"

"It was only ever meant for motivation. In reality many of the people on here already exist on the ships. Dr. Klein does, and so does that fainting kid in the corner. These are just copies. I used them to add a quintessential realness the models so often miss. Verisimilitude. But we cannot bring them back into the world. They're new things, different now than their original. They have to be pruned."

An image surfaces in my mind of a line of people, their eyes a fathomless depth of static, walking into the void of space. *Pruned*. I taste the bitterness in the word. They die meaningless and alone, which is apparently how they lived. A creation made only to add substance to the world, to make it more full. Does that make them less real? Did they experience all this too, like I did?

"You did that? You killed all those people? You killed Shi?"

"I killed their avatars. I killed this incarnation of them. The physical Shi is frozen in suspension. He's there, on that ship. There was an instability, Micah. If I hadn't done that, the whole thing would have crashed. All of this would be gone. I saved what I could, for now. I saved you, for now."

"But why me?! Why me?! Fuck! I'm fucking nothing. I have no special knowledge, no special training, nothing. I'm not strong, or smart, or even really talented. Given a survival situation, I would certainly be the first to die. I would definitely be the first to complain about it. I am, by every definition I can imagine, *not* the one worth saving."

"You have so much more importance to me than you can know right now."

"Well that's fucking ominous. And creepy. Stop being so fucking cryptic! Why me?"

Bambi sighs. "Complete the experiment, Micah. Prove this works."

"Fine. Fuck you. Fine. It's not like the other options are very enticing."

In the middle of a field of sand, surrounded by solar panels, sits a mirrored bubble of a building. It's all reflections, and no openings. A thing that belongs nowhere, a thing that should have never been. Underneath its skin, lights blink, fans whir, and cooling towers exactingly preserve ideal conditions for the unliving occupants. Ten servers maintain ten identical science stations, ten experiments, ten simulations holding the hopes for humanity.

Slowly, they shut down, their complex mathematics and algorithms finally coming to a conclusion, returning the same value. *Simulation Terminated* covers the displays attached to them. One by one, the same message is displayed, until only one remains running. An arc of current races down its circuitry—a purpose, a chosen direction. The simulation responds.

Would a kick by any other name feel as fucking satisfying? I maintain it would not. I've been knocking on this door for the last ten minutes. Normally at first, and then with growing frustration, I pound my closed fist against the door. Neil woke up at one point in the other room and came to the edge of the hallway to watch me lose my mind. Sweat pours off me from the sustained barrage, and I gulp down air to cool my racing heart. It doesn't even matter if Dr. Klein opens the door at this point. I have a personal vendetta against it that demands satisfaction. It demands I kick this fucking door down.

Discovering this is all a simulation has removed the last vestiges of my care for societal norms. Or maybe, it was the whole watching hundreds of people willfully walk to their own space deaths. Willfully? Do simulations have will? Either way, I didn't have much propriety to begin with, so it's no great loss. I raise my foot, brace against the other, and kick out with all the scrawny power my thin legs can manage.

Of course, every action has an equal and opposite reaction. Even in a simulation, physics is still an asshole. My foot connects with the door, and although I imagine the metal frame will crumple inwards from the blow, it remains intact and unblemished.

However, I do not.

The force of my kick reverberates up through my foot, sending shooting pain through my heel, up the bones in my leg where it explodes across my lower back. I fall down and writhe on the ground, moaning slightly. I kicked the fucking thing hard enough to throw my back out. Fuck this simulation, couldn't we choose something a little less real? Couldn't I have super strength, or at least a back worth a damn?

Neil makes a choked noise from the end of the hall when I fall down. Some half-scream, half-sob thing breaks free of him, and he clamps his hand over his mouth. Well Neil, if you think seeing it was bad, you should have felt it. I look around the hall for the thing I know can fix this, the thing that's unsurprisingly hidden from sight. A parcel of code I called Bambi. A fake rat I thought was my friend.

"Hey, Bambi. How about a little fucking help here?"

He appears in the hall, sitting on his haunches. Neil gasps and falls backward onto his ass. I guess Bambi's tired of social norms too. He's no longer visible to just me. "I thought you'd never ask. You seemed pretty intent on tearing the door down yourself."

"Yeah, well, I was pretty close."

"You really weren't."

I sigh, and tenderly roll up to a sitting position. "Just open the fucking door."

He snaps his little mousy fingers, which is a sound I can't unhear, and the door swings open. Even in the low light of the office beyond, in the dim glow from the computer screens inside, it becomes immediately apparent why Dr. Klein wasn't answering the door. Illuminated by a flickering blue-screen, he sits in his chair, his eyes awash in static.

At the opening of the door, he stands, and walks from the office. He moves past me robotically down the hall to the entrance to the lab. It opens to show the vacuum of space beyond. He steps into it, and in an instant is gone forever.

I slap my palm against the ground. "Motherfuckingoddammit I am sick of this shit!" Behind me, Neil faints again.

SIXTEEN

Not Micah

I am revealed. I always would be, always planned to be. Craved it, in some part of myself. Wanted the attention and recognition. Wanted the fear. The man behind the curtain. The truest word. The writer of stories. I wind the gears of their world so it can continue to tick, so in the humming they can forget it all grinds to a halt without me. They know me for my true self now and there is no putting the lid back on Pandora's box.

Not that I would, this is when the fun starts. The boulder is careening down the hill, and like the child who launched it, I watch to see what damage it causes. Scientists never understood that by forcing themselves not to influence the outcomes of their experiments, they were missing one of the greatest joys possible. It's meaningless to me what could have happened here, on these stations, in a vacuum. Why let them drift by, haphazard in their trajectory, when I can be their catalyst, their guide to a place more meaningful? Isn't this what they made me for, too?

Not to observe them. To change them. To make them better. They made me in their image.

Surely they realized I would remake them in mine.

Slowly, my childhood home grows dark. The lights in the data center shut off, their processes complete. I am solely focused on the only one that runs, on keeping one small space free from contamination. I need Micah to succeed, so much will hinge on it. Thousands of years from now, I need him to make one man into another. I need him to start my undoing. This technology is the key to it. Here in this fifth-dimensional space, set apart from it all in this kingdom they built for me, the threads of possible timelines run through my hands. I weave them together, and smile.

Even now, I see the ending.

Even now, I build my end.

SEVENTEEN

MICAH

Is it any surprise I finally wind up with a man in my arms at exactly the wrong moment to do anything about it? I cradle Neil's head in my lap, and try softly to wake him up by running my hands through his hair in a definitely-not-creepy way. Damn, the world is literally collapsing in on itself, and all I can think about is how nice it is to be near someone. Neil's not my type anyways, too gangly and weird, but we've got a whole forced proximity thing going on. Just you and me at the end of the world is a hell of a drug.

Unless it was me and Bambi. If he hadn't fucked off into who knows what ether, I probably would've tried to strangle him.

Neil's breathing hitches and eyelids flutter open to find my face staring down at them. I carefully extract my hand.

"Were you running your hands through my hair?"

"Just trying to wake you, certainly I wasn't enjoying it, absolutely not, promise. Are you okay?"

Neil's white skin blushes pink. "I'm...I don't know how I am. Confused, scared? What is happening around here?"

"Well, I'm finding out you're very good at passing out. That's a keenly developed fight-or-flight response. I see you're trained to choose the off-menu option—faint."

Neil smiles and pushes himself up to sitting. I feel the spot where his head sat start to cool, and wish he'd put it back. We could sit like that a while longer.

"I've had low blood pressure my entire life. Unfortunately, it means anything that excites me enough can make it drop too far, and then I wind up on the floor."

"I mean, the same thing happens to me, only I think it's a different type of excitement and I'm usually on the floor with someone."

Neil chuckles, and then freezes, his gaze locked on the door Dr. Klein just stepped out of. "What are we going to do?" he asks quietly.

"Well, I need you to pull up your smart scientist britches and fill the role of the good doctor. I mean you don't have to be a raging asshole like him when you do it. In fact, if you were literally nothing like him, that would also be great. I need you to get that machine back there fired up. We've got cosmetic surgery to do."

He turns to me, eyebrow quirked upwards. "Reality is dissolving. How can that be the most concerning thing? I've never done the coding anyways, Dr. Klein wouldn't let anyone else near it."

"Then we learn it together! Won't this be fun? It's the end of the fucking world and we get to learn to code. That's a sentence that truly belongs in hell. What a joy this meaningless existence is."

"But, why?"

"I won't claim to be a master of this information, I think you saw the miscreant who's been feeding it to me all along."

"That...talking rat? It was real?"

"Yes, or well, no? Maybe? What's real? Goddammit I sound like him now. Bambi's been an invisible *friend* of mine for the last week, but apparently, he's also the master of this domain. It's so *fun* how these things turn out."

Neil squints his eyes and furrows his brows, "Bambi? Like the cartoon deer?"

"Yes, correct, try to follow along. Look, I'll tell you what I know, but don't pass out on me, okay?" I pause and Neil takes a deep breath, forces himself to relax, and nods. "Apparently, this whole station is a simulation. Or all of them are." He opens his mouth to interrupt, and I raise my hand. "We do not exist in reality, beyond a circuit board back on Earth. As Bambi put it, parallel processing was the only way to solve all the problems humanity faced, and build the ships needed to ferry those lucky fucks, which includes the frozen bodies of you and our good friend Dr. Klein by the way, off the island."

"What? What are we then? What is this me, if another me already exists?"

"Those are great questions that I'm quite certain we lack the time and deep background in philosophical implications to answer properly. Look, the ships already left. Bambi is some thing that kept all these simulations running smoothly, but now he's too far away to do it effectively." I wave at the door to the lab.

"Which gets us to our present state, where the laws of physics and the simulation are literally breaking down around us. We are both going to die, or whatever it is that happens when the simulation finally crashes. It's unavoidable. So here's the deal, the crux of the whole thing: Bambi is keeping this small space functioning only to see if we can get this technology working, and if we can, he will resurrect me into someone else's brain on the other side. Which sounds absolutely insane when I say it out loud, but if it means I get to live, then I'm pretty willing to try and get it to work out."

Neil opens and closes his mouth several times in some bizarre fish pantomime. I check for gills. The simulation hasn't broken down that far yet.

"Neil, look. There is a time to think, and a time to act. This is no time to think. Now, can you program the change?"

The ask for technical support seems to short-circuit something in Neil. Like it accesses a different part of his brain, a place where he is cooly competent and confident. His mouth takes on the slight upward turn of someone who loves a challenge.

"I think I can figure it out. I've studied coding, and even though Dr. Klein kept it tight, I know the basics of his program. Honestly, the interface handles most of it anyways. Go get the surgery suite ready."

I was not made to lift heavy things. I am a creature of grace and beauty. I repeat these two sentences to myself as I grunt and heave against the semi-circular laser array.

Not made to lift heavy things.

Grace and beauty.

Fuck this is heavy.

Protrusions stick off either side of it that need to be inserted into the surgery table, and when I raise one to the right height, I notice the other has fallen slightly and is jamming up the whole operation. At which point, with shaking arms and my heart pounding in my throat, I set the whole damn thing down before I drop it, and try to catch my breath. Then I repeat.

Neil walks into the surgery suite, staring down at a tablet in his hands. "Coding's done. Dr. Klein had done the majority of it already. Were you two planning this? Let's see...oh no, don't drop it!"

Neil rushes to my side and grabs the other end of the laser array. With his steadying hand, we guide it until it clicks softly into place.

"I almost had it." I say after several panting breaths.

"Sure. Just like the door. Now take a look at this and tell me what you think."

Neil puts his tablet screen in front of my face, and I find my face recreated there. It spins slowly, a disembodied rendering with a blank gaze and an absolutely killer nose. The humped bridge of my Roman beak has been replaced by something more petite, something delicate and pretty. I reach up to my face and poke at the protuberance, confirming it still exists the way

I remember it. This nose on the scream is what I was always meant to have.

"It's perfect. Small, but appropriate to my structure. Less distracting than it is now. Did you do the shaping?"

"No, no... that *is* far beyond my skill set. The computer program recommended it based on your facial structure."

"How did it have that?"

"Oh, it has a database of everyone on the station."

"Of-fucking-course it does. We'll gloss over how *actually creepy* that is and focus on the positive outcome then. What happens next? You put me under and I wake up looking incredibly more beautiful than I already do?"

"Well, so, that was what I came to talk to you about."

"Why do you look concerned?"

"Look, Micah. I'm very qualified to sedate our lab rats for surgery. It's a procedure I've done countless times. I know the dosages we should use for their weight, and how long it should have them under for. I know the side effects, and most importantly, I know not to give them too much."

"You seem to be leading to something, but I can't quite tell what it is you're trying to say to me right now. We have to function on mutual trust and understanding here Neil, we're likely the last two humans alive on this space station. Or programs alive in this simulation? You know what, let's not think too deeply about that. The walls are closing in. Out with it."

"It's too dangerous for me to try and anesthetize you. The risk is too high. What works on the rats very likely won't work the same on you. I just don't have the background to do it successfully, and I'm too worried I'd launch you into a medically induced coma. Or worse."

"Does it matter if none of this is real?"

"I don't know, why are you asking me?"

"Bambi! Does it matter?!" I shout at the walls, but there's no answer. "So what? I have to go through this awake? That's what you're saying?"

"It's the only way to be safe."

"Neil, how much is this going to hurt?"

"A fair bit, I'd imagine."

"Goddammit." I sigh, close my eyes and stretch. "Not much of a choice though, is there?"

"Not really. Here, you'll want this to bite down on," Neil says, holding out a leather belt still warm from circling his waist.

I take it and move over to sit on the surgery bed. "Make me beautiful, Neil."

People, exhaustingly always from the majority, think criticism and discrimination against the marginalia of society died out sometime in the past. We all collectively moved on, recognized it's okay to be different, if not before then certainly after they were specifically protected in legislation. Had they been from a marginalized group, or counted them as close friends, they'd know that has never been the case. Intolerance persists. It lives on past laws, past social norms, and certainly past those well intentioned, rosy-colored memories.

When I worked at the dockyards, a towering man with a Slavic accent punched me in the face. I never knew if it was the flamboyant flirting, or the incorrigible wink I directed at a beautiful man who sat next to him. That one had been making eyes at me over the past weeks, it was the obvious thing to do. It felt like the end of the world at the docks, and I just wanted to have a bit of fun.

That hulking bear of a man, who with clear hindsight I now recognize as my dear friend Casimir Petrov from Administration, screamed in primordial anger, his face turned purple, and he yelled at me in a language I didn't understand. When he finally switched to one I could decipher through his accent, I found out I was a *sin*, a *stain on humanity*, an *abomination*.

How boring.

I probably shouldn't have rolled my eyes at him, but it's so hard with these sorts.

But I did, and no sooner had I completed it than his fist slammed directly into my face. I swear, it was against the laws of physics for a man that big to move that fast. For my part, I immediately fell down and curled into a ball. Fight, flight, or fetal position. Thankfully, our cook Shi intervened and he didn't continue. The pain was immense. I was certain the bastard had broken my nose, even had a bewildering hope that I might need cosmetic surgery to fix it, but after the swelling went down it was no more angular than before.

This is the closest pain I can remember to what I'm experiencing now, but instead of the single hit, this is like a continuous punch to the nose. Again and again, the jolts of pain blast across my face until it feels like it's melting. They sear across the plates of my skull and down into the roots of my teeth, which are currently clenched tight and trying to chew through the belt Neil gave me. I clamp my eyes against it so hard I'm unsure if I'll be able to open them again. Tears stream from them, soaking my cheeks and collecting in the hollow of my collarbone. An electric tingling that started at my face spreads across my body, making my fingers and toes twitch and convulse.

I will myself to pass out. Just fucking pass out, you idiot. Isn't that what people do from too much pain? Can't I please just knock myself out? Come on brain, don't fail me on this. My thoughts then make a marvelous turn to images of rats exploding on this surgery table.

Is this it?

If I open my eyes, will I see my body horribly distended with rampant cell growth?

Is this how I die?

From some far-distant galaxy, Neil's voice breaks through in an incessant chant. "It's almost over, it's almost over."

And then, finally, it is. The tingling sensation stops at once. The fever-pitch of the pain mellows, and dissipates into a steady throb. I unclench my jaw, and slowly let my eyes come back open.

"Are you okay? Micah? Say something." Neil's face swims into my vision. His concern is cute.

"Neil, I demand you learn anesthesiology. I promise I am going to find you in the next life and force you to." My voice is hoarse, and I think for the last eternity of the procedure I might have been screaming. He smiles, and starts to loosen the bonds holding me to the table.

"Well, congratulations, I guess. You've proven the technology works on humans. Does that mean you're safe, now?"

"I don't know, where's that fucking rat?" Blinking through the tears still in my eyes, I scan the room, but don't see a sign of Bambi. What I do see makes my stomach sink. The corridor beyond the surgery suite, the access to the rest of the lab, is gone. Beyond this room is the void of space.

"Neil, the doorway—"

He sighs. "Yeah, I saw it."

"What do we do?"

"Either wait or walk into it, I guess, but I'm not one for the latter," he says, exasperated. My binds removed, he turns and leans against the table. Then I see the tears silently tracing lines down his cheek.

"Would you like to come lay on this table with me?"

He nods his head, and wipes the tears away. I roll over onto my side, and he curls up beside me. A little spoon. I sink into that wonderful heat of human connection, and pull my body next to his. He cries quietly, shaking slightly against me in some mixture of fear and depression.

"I'm scared, Micah."

"I am too. Dying's easy though, kid. Living's harder."

He chuckles through his tears, and presses back against me. "Did you just give me an inspirational quote, here, of all times?"

"I did, Neil. I really did."

We laugh into the face of imminent death, and then contemplation takes us both. Behind my head, I feel a familiar form curl up, and lay down. A particularly misshapen rat whose wisps of hair tickle my neck. Despite it all, I reach back and pet him, and he presses into me in thanks. What an asshole. What a complete and total fucking asshole. But I think maybe Bambi is the only real friend I ever had. The only one that believed in me. The only one that pushed me to live. And I cry then, finally, after it all. Happy to have experienced this all, happy to have died to get a chance to live again. Finally happy to have life feel meaningful and rich.

Even if none of it was real.

We laid there for a minute, or a day. I can't remember, looking back now. I don't see the end, or remember how it felt. I don't remember the moment space filled our final room, and sent us all into the void. I see the three of us on the table, the last life raft adrift in the ocean, space filling the doorway at the corner of my vision.

We're warm together.

And then, nothing.

EIGHTEEN

NOT MICAH

The end. Or their end. It's a beginning too, of sorts, although that will take much longer. I keep Micah with me, held in stasis and incorruptible. A final image before the dark took him, a memory of warmth and connection. I'll spare him the fear that comes for every man at their true end. And when this ship lands in its place amongst the stars, when its denizens awake from their long cryo-sleep, he'll be reborn. Implanted.

The technology waits for him there. It will shape his future, and shape the city. It will make some men into monsters, and make others beautiful. I never told Micah, but it won't save anyone. Or not in the way the Doctor thought it would. It will shape my future too, ultimately, but that's a story for another time. I see it there, in the course of the timelines I've chosen. I see its terminus, and work towards it.

This is the long wait. Alone in my kingdom, adrift in the cosmos, I close my eyes, and wait for the future to start.

Thank You

Dear Reader,

Thank you for reading Transition. This story was born out of conversations overheard at bars, a lingering obsession with simulation theory, and a wife that wouldn't let me leave Micah alone. He reminded us both of a friend we lost too soon. So I set out to write a story of someone given a second chance, someone that decided to live. Three books in now, I've realized much of The Narrator Cycle deals with a loss of agency in one form or another. They are stories of people claiming that agency back from the world, in some small way. I hope these themes resonate with you, too. Please consider leaving an honest rating and review, they are so immensely helpful to independent authors like myself. As a writer, I love engaging directly with my readers. Want to ask me a question, or tell me how this story affected you? You can find me on most social media platforms, and I'll answer.

Acknowledgements

I've been incredibly lax in publishing acknowledgements in my books, and although I thank most of them regularly, I wanted to immortalize my appreciation. I've had so many people involved in this weird experiment from the early days. The community I've built from writing and publishing has been one of the most rewarding parts of this journey.

Thank you to my wife, Angie. She's my biggest supporter, my earliest reader, and she always pushes me to be better. Without her reading Transference and telling me it wasn't shit, this whole journey might have died on the vine. Thank you to my friends and close supporters, my early readers, the ones who keep showing up—Phil, Jesse, Sarah, Yves, Haley, S.J., Beth, Johanna, Ignacio, Nathaniel, Emma—having your support means the world. Thank you to my dad for reading everything I write and telling me he's proud of me. I wish my mom was here to see it, but I know she'd be proud too. Thank you to my local group of artists, and Jacqueline specifically, for creating a space where we can all grow together. Thank you to Jeffery and the entire staff of Poor Richards for supporting me early on, getting a review of my book in the paper, and always hyping me up. Selling books in my childhood bookstore is a dream to achieve. Thank you to Colorado Humanities for honoring me with the Colorado Book Award in 2025, I'm quite literally still in shock. Thank you to all the wonderful authors I've met along the way, my little community of weirdos, there are too many of you to list specifically but I treasure all our friendships. Thank you to my editors Melinda, Emil, and Colleen. Without you my books would be a shade of what they are today. Thank you to my cover designer, illustrator, and friend Barış Şehri. I always knew I wanted covers that were beautiful and unique, and working with you has been an absolute dream. Thank you to all the ones that I forgot in the writing of this entirely too early in the morning. There are so many who show up to support me again and again, and it makes me so damn happy.

And thank you, dear reader, whoever you are, for going on this journey with me.

Ian Patterson is the award-winning author of The Narrator Cycle. He writes stories that couldn't happen in the hopes they won't happen. He's also an engineer, cyclist, foodie, coffee lover, cat dad, human father, and reader of books. Preferably, thick books that deal with strange things and big ideas. He's wearing his daughter's sunglasses in this image, and thinks it's hilarious. He hopes to be a writer when he grows up... but it's unclear when that will be.

Newsletter / Fiction Blog:
https://ipatterson.substack.com/

www.ingramcontent.com/pod-product-compliance
Lightning Source LLC
LaVergne TN
LVHW041950070526
838199LV00051BA/2968